My Spy

By

ALYSIA S. KNIGHT

Heart Dreams PRESS

My Spy
By Alysia S. Knight
Published by Heart Dreams Press
Copyright © 2015 Heart Dreams Press
Cover design: by Kelli Ann Morgan @
www.inspirecreativeservices.com

The views expressed within this work are the sole responsibility of the author and do not represent Heart Dreams Press or any of its affiliates.

This is a work of fiction. Names, characters, place and events are product of the author's imagination. Any similarities to actual persons, living or dead, business establishments or events are purely coincidental.

ISBN:1-942000-13-8
ISBN-13:978-1-942000-13-6

Also available from Alysia S. Knight

ൟ

Past To Die For

ൟ

Temperature Rising

ൟ

Kare for Me

ൟ

Blind Witness

ൟ

Beauty and the Chief

ൟ

Trail to Her Heart

ൟ

His Governess

ൟ

Her Brand of Trouble

ൟ

The Ruins – Out of Time

To my husband, Merle.
Thanks for sharing the trip to Thailand and
Angkor Wat with me. Besides the book, it
gave me many great memories.
I will miss our adventures together.
Love you forever,
Alysia S. Knight

Chapter One

"You can't be serious. That's right out of some old spy novel." Thayne Rees looked at Matt Harding, his friend and boss, and shook his head.

"That's how he wants it. I think the drama appeals to him." Matt shrugged.

"But James Bond Island? Really?"

"Hey, just think of it as a vacation on us before you retire."

Thayne grimaced. "Last time you gave me a vacation, I got shot."

"I told you, we were given bad intel."

"And now we have a guy who wants to play secret agent, and you wonder why I want to retire."

Matt leaned forward, steepling his fingers. "You still certain?"

"Absolutely." He could see Matt getting his arsenal of arguments ready and decided to cut him off. "I can't do it anymore. I need a change and have decided it's time to put my engineering degree to use."

"You already do that," Matt pointed out.

"I mean full time. It's time Matt, and you know it."

"It's time you found a woman."

Thayne shifted in his seat, surprised that Matt would bring that up. He was one of the few people who knew he'd been married once before and what happened to his wife.

"I'm not going there again," Thayne said flatly.

"You know the odds of something happening again—"

"I'm not going to take the risk," he said in finality that ended Matt's argument.

"Okay. Look, this is just a simple pickup with a bit of melodrama."

"There's no such thing as a simple pickup and you know it. When you think it's easy, that's when you get dead."

"Now who's being over-dramatic?"

Thayne arched an eyebrow at him.

"Okay," Matt conceded the point. "But, the thing is, they really want this information and are paying well for it. So we go with the plan." Matt leaned forward.

"Why don't they send one of their guys?"

"They were told to keep out of sight by higher ups. Total hands off. This is their way around it."

Thayne rolled his eyes and shook his head. "What the other hand doesn't know."

"Exactly. Look you get to go hang out at some of the most beautiful beaches in the world, get some sun, take a boat tour out to incredible island formations and buy a fridge magnet. Then you hang out a couple more days and come home. In ten days, you're living the boring life of the retired man of leisure, playing with your inventions."

Chapter Two

"Oh," Emma cried out as the boat shifted just as she started to step down. She pitched forward, slipping off the seat.

"Easy, I've got you." The deep male voice sounded as strong male arms locked around her, pulling her into a firmly muscled chest, lightly dusted with golden hair.

She gasped again as she locked her hands on the flexed biceps to steady herself. "Sorry," she exclaimed.

"Don't apologize. It's been a long time since I've had a beautiful woman fall into my arms."

Emma felt a blush burn her cheeks though she knew he was teasing her. She looked up and all thoughts flew from her mind. The man had the most striking blue eyes she had ever seen, surrounded by incredibly long, thick lashes. A lot of women were jealous of her naturally long lashes but his put hers to shame.

A twinkle flashed in the blue depth, and Emma realized she was still holding on to him. Still she couldn't seem to force herself to let go. She felt fused in place then a bag hit her in the back.

"Can you take this, Emma?" Paige stood on the seat by the engines waiting. People were lined up behind her.

"Oh, sure. Sorry." Emma blushed even more. "Thank you." She released him and turned back to her friend, relieved when she felt him move away. She took the bag as Paige put her hand on her shoulder and stepped down into the boat.

"Nice catch," Paige whispered. "I knew you had it in you. We just had to get you out of your hidey-hole life.

"What?" Emma failed to follow her.

Paige smirked. "Catching the best looking guy on the boat." Paige looked past her and grinned. "Correction, make that probably the best looking man on the island. Wow. You've got to love a guy with a slight cleft in his chin."

Emma couldn't stop herself from glancing toward the front of the big speed boat. The man was saying something to one of the tour helpers. He did have a cleft in his chin and when he smiled there was a dimple in his cheek.

Paige was right. He was one good looking guy. Instead of the shaggy or scruffy look, with a slight growth of beard, he was clean shaven. Paige was wrong though, there was absolutely no way she could catch the interest of a man like that. He was so out of her league, she couldn't even dream of him noticing her. He was just being nice. He ducked down where the canopy ended at the windshield and went out into the sun on the front of the boat, stopping to talk to a couple out there.

"Come on." Paige nudged her. "Let's go sit up front." Paige took her backpack and stepped past before Emma could answer.

Paige had already removed her swimsuit cover to reveal her bikini and staked her spot about a foot and a half from the man. She'd placed her pack on the seat next to her by the other couple so, if Emma wanted to sit by her, she had no choice but to sit by him. For a moment, she debated staying under the canopy then she heard Paige.

"I'm Paige and this is Emma." Paige motioned to her and Emma gave up and stepped forward.

"I'm Laura, this is my husband Alec." The woman next to Paige said with a heavy Aussie accent.

"Where are you from?" Emma asked, settling on the

seat, trying to ignore the man beside her.

"Melbourne," the woman with short tasseled, brown hair said.

"I loved Melbourne. I went there with my parents a few years ago," Emma answered.

"So on vacation?" Laura asked.

"For my mother and I, yes. My father was on business. He's an engineering manager and was doing business with an auto company there. While he worked, my mother and I wandered all over the city. We walked to the botanical gardens, harbor, along the river and, of course, to the market."

"So you enjoyed it."

"Immensely, it was great. The people there were so friendly."

"What about you?" Paige leaned forward to see around Emma to her rescuer from the fall.

"I love Melbourne, too." He grinned. "Plan to go back there some time for pleasure."

"You've been there then?" Paige asked.

"Several times on business. My name's Thayne."

"You're from the U.S.?" Emma asked, finally getting the nerve to look at him. She felt her breath catch again.

"Yes. San Diego."

"Really," Paige exclaimed excitedly. "Emma's from there."

Emma wanted to clamp her hand over her friend's mouth. She knew Paige well enough to know there was no way now she could resist match-making. She sent Paige a quick look which her friend totally ignored.

"Is that so?"

Emma could feel his eyes on her. She tried not to groan and fought down a blush, hoping her tan hid evidence that always appeared when she was in the presence of an attractive man. Well, not any man, just ones that interested her. Not that she was interested, she tried to tell herself. He was just so good looking.

"Yes." She turned to meet his gaze. "I ... we grew up in Laguna Hills but moved to San Diego about six months ago." She tried not to get lost in those probing blue eyes. She could swear he could see right into her.

"You still live in Laguna?" He looked past her to Paige.

Emma wished she could change her places. Paige was a pretty and petite pixie. She was an outgoing, people person, with a bubbly, friendly personality that pulled people in. Paige was the type that someone like him would be attracted to. Definitely not an average nerd like she was.

Emma tried to be realistic. She conceded to the fact she was quite pretty but her people skills, okay man skills, were seriously lacking.

"No," Paige answered. "I grew up there, but I'm going to be living in Bangkok for the next year, teaching English. Emma came to help me get settled. After four days in Bangkok, we went to Siam Reap to see Angkor Wat, which was amazing, then came down here."

"Enjoying it?" he asked glancing at Paige then looked back to her.

"Yes." Paige continued on. "We went snorkeling two days ago at Phi Phi Island. It was great. I think this should be just as good."

"My husband and I are thinking of doing that tour," Laura spoke up.

"You really should," Paige urged.

Emma forced her attention to the Australian couple. "I agree. If you do go, something you might try is what one of the guys on the boat showed us. Take a piece of pineapple with you into the water, that hard core area in the center. We did it and the fish went crazy over it. They came up and nibbled it right out of our fingers. We had fifty to a hundred fish swarming around us. All colors, shapes and sizes. It was so amazing."

"Thanks for the hint." Laura looked excited as did her husband.

Conversation broke off as more people came out on the front, and they had to slide closer together. The guide addressed everyone, and the boat got underway. Slow at first, it allowed everyone easy access to take pictures. Everyone turned, watching as they passed other boats and a small island, then the boat picked up speed until it skimmed rapidly over the water.

Emma was aware of Thayne beside her, his leg brushing hers. She felt a moment of relief when he stood then he grabbed hold of the bottom of his shirt and pulled it up and off. Her breath caught and heart pounded at the expanse of tanned muscle just inches from her. He wasn't bodybuilder built, but lean, hard, strong muscle that shimmered in the sun, calling to be touched. She noticed a faint scar on his side under his arm then he settled down beside her, and she forgot everything as she felt the warmth of his skin next to her.

Emma chided herself at the awareness she felt. She tried to tell herself the heat was just from the hot, humid air, but she knew it wasn't. The man had a powerful feel about him that set off her senses.

She turned in the seat, letting the wind hit her in the face in an attempt to cool down. Emma didn't know what was the matter with her? She'd never reacted to a man like this. She tried to block him from her mind but it was like he'd captured a spot there.

Shifting, she focused on the small green islands that jutted out of the water with thick foliage and rocky cliffs. They were so beautiful. She brought her camera up and took several pictures.

"So you're enjoying yourself?" His voice sounded close to her ear.

She turned her head to answer and got lost in his eyes. They were bluer than the water they were cruising over.

The boat hit a wake left by another boat jostling her. Emma almost slipped off the seat. His arm went out around her, pinning her in place.

"You're determined to fall off yet."

"I wasn't expecting the bump," she got out. "The water's been so smooth."

"It's beautiful." His eyes caressed over her like he was saying she was beautiful.

"Yes."

"Have you been enjoying yourself?" he repeated his earlier question.

"Yes. What about you?"

"Yes." He smiled. "I flew in a couple days ago. Hung out at the beach the first day, then took a tour of the island, trying to acclimatize and get on the time schedule here."

"I've done better with that than I was afraid I would."

"Yeah, you'll probably find going home a bit harder."

"Great, I tend to wake up at five o'clock in the morning." She gave a half-laugh.

"Nothing wrong with being an early riser. The beach is peaceful then."

"You walked on the beach that early?"

He shrugged. "There wasn't anything else to do. Maybe I'll see you next time."

Emma decided she didn't want to press that but couldn't keep back the other question that hit her. "You're alone?"

"I have been for a long time."

Emma felt as if the words had slipped out from deep within him – that Thayne hadn't really meant to say them. The words also made her want to reach for him, to comfort him, which was totally silly because self-assuredness radiated off the man.

❧

Thayne couldn't believe what he'd revealed about himself. It wasn't like him to let things slip. Then again, he couldn't believe how drawn he was to Emma.

He knew he should get up and move. The back of the boat being completely full was the excuse he made to himself, and it was true, but Thayne knew the real reason he didn't move was he just didn't want to leave Emma's side. He couldn't leave her. It felt too good to talk to her, to feel her body alongside his.

"What do you do?" he asked.

"I'm a teacher."

"English?"

"No. I'm a speech pathologist."

"Really, I don't think I've ever met a speech pathologist before. What exactly do you do?" Thayne studied how the sun played over her, accenting the tan he'd bet didn't come from a tanning bed.

"I actually have two jobs. One part time in the school. I work with children that have speech problems. The other, I work in the hospital with people that have had a severe trauma or stroke, something that affects their speech. I do what I can to make it better."

"It sounds interesting." He liked the sound of what she did, and it seemed to fit her.

"It can be."

The boat hit another wake and he instinctively reached to steady her.

"Thanks." She looked over at him and smiled.

He was close enough that, though her hair was pulled back into a thick braid that ran down her back, he could still see golden streaks of light in her hair that was too brown to be called blonde but too blonde to be brown. He'd bet the gold was natural. Nature seemed to love her. Kneeling up on the bench with the water behind her and the sun glowing down was a perfect setting for her.

She turned facing forward, letting the wind hit her in the face.

"You like boating." It was a statement not a question.

She glanced over her shoulder at him. "Yes, but I don't get to do it often. Yesterday, the water was too rough, and we were going too fast to stand. Look at the islands. Aren't they amazing how they just thrust right out of the water? Wow."

Her eyes were bright with excitement and a beautiful blue that were like pools inviting a man to dive into. He wasn't going there, he reminded himself and pulled back literally and figurative.

They chatted with everyone as the boat bucked over the water. The boat came around an island and the driver cut the motor. There were several other boats similar to theirs, and a big boat with a stack of inflated canoes on the back. More canoes filled the water and were paddled toward them as they drifted to a stop about forty feet from the island.

"This must be our first stop," Paige said beside her.

"Yes, look there's the cave in the cliff. They look like stalactites hanging down." Emma reached down and pulled up her swimsuit cover, bringing it up over her head.

Thayne forgot all about his moment of self-declaration.

She wore a one piece swimsuit, but with the sides cut away, hiding nothing of Emma's shape, which was amazing. Her long, lean lines flared out in all the right places. She wasn't overly built, just perfect. His arms would fit nicely around her, and when he held her, he'd know he was holding a woman.

The guide started giving instructions and calling numbers for groups of two or three to get into the canoes as they pulled up behind the boat.

Thayne had to force his eyes from Emma as she moved in front of him in the line. He wanted to wrap his hand around her braid and draw her back to him and capture those smiling lips of hers. He was debating on bribing Paige to trade spots with him, when the woman did it for him.

"I'll go with Michael." Paige stepped back by the man from England. "You go with Thayne. That will make the canoes more even."

Unfortunately, the guide stopped the exchange before it could be made, calling the women into a canoe with a teenage girl, whose other family members were in the canoe in front of them.

Paige looked back and shrugged, as if to say, 'sorry, I tried'. Thayne wondered just what she was trying. Was she really matchmaking her friend with a total stranger. Thayne wasn't sure what to think.

Once again, he decided he'd better get his mind back on business, but he watched as Emma stepped carefully into the canoe, in front of Paige but behind the teenager. When she placed her feet up on the inflated sides he was rewarded with a view of delicate feet tipped with pink painted toenails.

Her canoe pushed off and was replaced with one for him and Michael. As soon as they were loaded, they were gliding over the water toward the cave under the island.

Monkeys stood on the rocks at the entrance. He took several pictures of them but, though he tried not to, his attention stayed focused on Emma. She leaned forward to say something to the girl, turned to take pictures of the monkeys on the other side, then pointed to a monkey that was carrying a baby and took several more pictures.

The guides paddled farther into the cave and it grew darker. His guide turned on the light strapped to his helmet and pointed it at the ceiling, illuminating bats hanging down. Thayne looked at the creatures then turned back to check on Emma's reaction. She showed no fear or revulsion. She raised her camera to click a picture, laughing at Paige who made a "eww," that was loud enough that he heard it.

As they continued into the cave, the ceiling got lower. Stalactites hung down. Thayne ducked then had to lie back entirely as the space between the water and the ceiling dropped to only a couple feet. Ahead of them light shown in but with the high tide, it was impossible to make it through. The cavern grew smaller due to a large piece of stone hanging down, taking up the center, causing a traffic jam of canoes as they all tried to maneuver around to go back out the way they came in.

His canoe bumped into another and he turned to lock gazes with Emma. "Fun?"

She nodded.

They bumped again. He reached over to help them shift and his hand came down on hers. A charge of awareness seared across his nerves in a way that made his heart leap.

Her lips formed a little 'O' that made him think she had felt it to then a stroke of the paddle forced them apart. A few minutes later, he was back at the mouth of the cave with the monkeys. One pulled back its lips and let out a sound that for some reason, Thayne thought that it was laughing at him.

He figured he deserved a good chastisement. What was he thinking? He was on a job. And even if he wasn't, there was no way he was going to be interested in the woman. He wasn't into vacation flings, and he certainly wasn't into long term relationships.

Reaching the boat, he got out but instead of returning to the front like he should have, he waited for Emma.

The teenager came first. Thayne helped her down then Emma came up past the big triple motors. He held out his hand to help her up, daring his hand to feel anything unusual.

She looked surprised and cautious as she placed her hand in his. Awareness hit him again then deepened as her eyes widened and she met his gaze. She froze and her fingers picked up a slight tremble. Her lips parted, and he thought of it as an invitation he was tempted to take.

"Would you like a drink?" The guide asked behind him. Thayne was about to answer yes when he realized the man hadn't been asking about Emma's lips.

Breaking the spell, Emma looked away from him. She released his hand making it past the engine and down off the bench.

"Yes, please." She sounded breathless.

"Coke, Sprite or Fanta?"

"I'll try Fanta," she said.

"Me, too." Thayne wasn't sure why he said it when he was handed a bottle of orange soda.

They went back to the front of the boat, but Paige stayed back talking.

"I don't think I've had this since I was a kid." He looked at Emma.

"I haven't either." She took a sip and smiled.

He took a swig. "Not bad."

She laughed. "I've noticed the soft drinks taste different over here. I like them better. I don't drink much pop at home."

"A wine girl?" he speculated. He didn't drink much alcohol, occupational hazard as far as he was concerned.

"No, a water girl." She waited as if expecting a derogatory comment.

"That's good."

She relaxed.

"So what did you think of the cave?" He leaned toward her as the boat started up.

"Wonderful."

"The bats didn't seem to bother you." He watched her face.

Light sparkled in her eyes. "No. Now if they all started flying, maybe, but as it was, it was pretty cool."

"You are the adventurous type."

She shrugged. "Again, it depends. I like to see new places, hike, snorkel, so on, but not the crazy stuff."

"Like?" he probed.

"Bungee jumping. There's no way," she said firmly.

"What about parasailing?"

"I'd like to try that sometime."

"I see. So crazy, but not insane."

She laughed again. Happiness radiated from her.

"You're not afraid of heights?"

"Not really. I did the Sydney bridge climb when in Australia."

"Really? I did it too." He wondered if she was there when he'd been. Even if she had been she'd been young. It made him realize he had about ten years on her. He had no business flirting with her, not that he was flirting. He was passing the time.

"So what category do you fit in?"

Thayne had to back up his brain to get what she was asking. "I think I fit in the crazy category now, but for a long time I was in the insane." He hadn't meant to add the end.

"Bungee jumping?"

"No, but it's amazing I survived a few things."

"Really, like what?" She leaned in.

Thayne had the urge to slide his arm around her and decided he was letting things get a little out of hand. "Just stupid stuff. Nothing to change the world."

"But at the time?" she asked way too perceptive.

"At the time, it seemed the only thing to do. Take a look at that." He pointed to an island coming up on the right, using it to change the subject.

Emma turned and pulled up her camera, taking a picture. "This is incredible. I can't believe it." She glanced back at him. "Mind if I ask why you're here alone?"

"Mainly, I'm here on business and taking some time to enjoy myself."

"Do you travel a lot?"

"I used to, but I'll be changing jobs soon, so I won't be

traveling as much. Though, I figure I'll still do some. There are a lot of places I'd like to see."

He could see the questions coming, but was saved when their boat came around, and they got their first look at James Bond Island with the small thumb-like rock that jutted out just off shore that made it so recognizable. The guide eliminated any further conversation by starting to tell about it.

Thayne took the chance to move away, asking himself once again what he was thinking spending so much time with her. He wasn't there to meet a woman. He didn't want to meet a woman. Matt's words about needing a woman came back to haunt him.

Thayne firmed his jaw. He was there to work, pick up the chip and that was it.

Chapter Three

"Isn't this cool?" Paige squealed. "They actually filmed a James Bond movie here."

Emma felt a touch of excitement herself. It was spectacularly beautiful. The small beach they pulled up to was packed with boats. A second later, she stepped off the back of the boat into the warm water and walked up the beach to a large sign under an overhang that almost made a cave.

"Where's Thayne?" Paige asked.

"I..." Emma looked around not seeing him. "I don't know. He must've gone exploring." She felt oddly bereft. "Where'd you go?" She turned her attention to Paige.

"I thought you might like some time alone to get to know him."

"Funny." Emma made a face.

"I'm serious. He's a good looking man and seems nice." Paige put her hands on her hips, defensively.

"I am not picking up a man in Thailand." Emma met her challenge.

"Come on, he's from San Diego, and you'll need someone to hang out with for the couple days after I'm gone."

"No. I don't know him. I can't believe you're even suggesting that."

Paige gave her a sly smile. "Then get to know him. He's interested."

"Well, what if I'm not?"

Paige's expression turned into a smirk. "This is me you're talking to. You're interested. You're just so locked up in being the good girl you can't loosen up and give him a chance."

"I say again, I don't know him."

"Well, my man meter says he's okay. And you know I'm pretty good at picking out questionable men."

"Yes, but that doesn't mean I'm going to risk anything out here. Besides, I'm waiting for the right man, and there's nothing wrong with that," Emma said. "Now." She raised her hand to halt Paige's continued argument. "Let's go see the island."

They climbed the path that led up into the trees, which would take them to the other, more famous, beach. Along the way views opened up of the rock island jutting out of the water. They stopped to take pictures as did the others in the group.

Breaking out of the foliage they found themselves on the famous beach with a crowd and a line of small souvenir stands. Emma ignored it all and wandered around taking pictures.

In her mind, she saw it like it was in the movie, a touch of mystical paradise. Unfortunately, she knew there was no hidden base inside the rock. Still it was amazing. Time seemed to fly by when the call went out for ten minutes to departure time.

"I want to get something." Paige headed for a stand under a brightly colored flag.

Emma took a couple more pictures before joining her. The woman at the booth was putting something in a bag.

"You ought to get something." Paige said.

"Why?"

"Really? Because it's James Bond Island."

"I don't..." She broke off.

Paige was shaking her head. "What about a magnet?"

"I can get one back in…" She broke off again. "How much?" She looked at the woman.

The woman quoted a price that was twice what she knew she could get it for in town.

"Oh, no. Thanks."

"Emma, come on. Get it." Paige must've known what she was thinking because she continued. "Think. It's James Bond Island. When you get back to San Diego you'll wish you had."

Emma wavered.

"You're from San Diego?" The woman at the booth leaned forward, as if taken by surprise.

"Yes." Emma pulled back a little as the woman reached out a hand toward her.

"And you came on the blue boat?" she asked, showing a smile with a missing tooth.

"Yes." Emma wondered what the woman seemed so interested in.

"San Diego, USA?" the woman said, her look growing more intense.

"Yes." Emma wasn't sure what else to say.

"You do not want that one. For you, San Diego, I have this one." She pulled out a magnet from under the table and held it out. It didn't look any different than the others. "Fifteen baht," the woman said.

Surprised, Emma handed over the money and slipped the magnet into the wrist pouch that she wore to keep her money and room key in. "Thank you." She dipped her head and the woman made the motion back, placing her hands together, in the way Emma was growing used to seeing the Thai people do.

Paige caught her arm. "I want one more picture. Will you get me by the cliff?"

Emma let Paige draw her away, still confused about what had just happened.

૱૱

Thayne flinched as the old woman at the booth said "San Diego" as if she was announcing it to the world. He wanted to shake his head and lecture the person who had hired her to pass the magnet. Then again, maybe that was the woman's idea of discreet.

Thayne felt a wave of frustration and guessed maybe he should have come there first. But his instinct was to be cautious, to get the lay of the area, and find out if anyone was watching. He wanted to know who the players were. Now he didn't know what to think.

He watched from behind a group of people on the other side of the next stand. He didn't believe in coincidence. So what did that say about Emma going to the stand and mentioning she was from San Diego and getting the magnet he was to receive?

He had no doubt she'd just received the one meant for him. Thayne didn't like it. He didn't like it at all. Especially, when he added that she interested him like no woman had in a long time.

Was it a set up? He had no answer, but he was going to find out. He stepped up to the stand and handed the woman money for a magnet, picking up a magnet like the one Emma had received, then angled his way so he would intersect with Emma on the way to the trail.

Paige saw him first. "Hey. Did you enjoy the island?"

"Yeah, though it could use a few less people for me."

She laughed. "It is crowded. It's hard to believe it's not the busy season."

"Looks like you got a souvenir." He pointed to the bag she carried.

"A braided shell bracelet. Emma got a magnet. She collects them."

Emma winced slightly. The motion that was totally believable as discomfort for something sounding lame.

"Nothing wrong with that," he said.

She eased at his comment.

"My grandmother had spoons from all over," he added.

Emma smiled. "Mine had salt shakers. Magnets don't take much space and are useful, though. Mine are really just more of a collage."

He accepted the answer, wondering if it really was true.

"Next, we head to the fishing village for lunch," Paige spoke up. "Do you want to join us, if we're not already divided into groups?"

"I'd love to." Thayne let his eyes drift to Emma. He debated if the flush that came over her was from the sun or his attention. If she was playing him, she was doing an incredible job of it. He didn't know any actress that could have pulled the performance off any more convincingly.

She had just the right amount of shyness to her. Though, it seemed sort of odd for someone so pretty and accomplished, on Emma it seemed believable. He just wasn't sure if he could. He glanced at the two inch wide band with a zipper pouch at her wrist and wondered how he was going to get the magnet from her.

"We'd better get back to the boat," Emma said.

Thayne motioned for them to go before him. Paige went first and he fell in behind Emma, enjoying the view of the sway of her hips. She had a beautiful, trim body. He wondered how long her hair would be if he freed it from the braid. As it was, it reached the middle of her back. He pulled his thoughts away from her figure.

Was her trip there on the boat a coincidence or a set up? What about the looks she gave him? The way she appealed to him. Was she meant to be intriguing to him and if so, how would someone know what appealed to him? She was nothing like his wife, who had been self-assured to the point of being forceful.

They had sometimes clashed because they both had been too dominant. In fact, he had wondered sometimes if the only reason they got along was because he was gone as much as he was. It was unfair of him, but he couldn't help speculate if he and Beth would have burned their love out.

He had never told anyone that, but it had already been on his mind back then. Beth's, too. That's why she had followed him on his assignment, to surprise him and try to rekindle some of their romance.

He shoved the thought away and concentrated on the woman in front of him. She was so – captivating. He'd been in this line of work too long not to be suspicious of her picking the magnet, especially with the biggest question of all being, her interest in him.

"I want one more picture," Emma announced abruptly stopping on the side of the trail and handing her camera to Paige. She climbed up on a rock in front of where the vegetation opened to give a great view. She smiled for the camera and Paige took the picture.

"Will you take one with me?" Thayne pulled his phone out and handed it to Paige, stepping up by Emma.

They smiled for the camera and Paige took the shot. "Come on, you need to make it better than that," Paige encouraged.

Thayne took the prompt, turning to Emma. He slipped his arm around her. She gasped when he pulled her closer.

"Smile sweetheart," he said low, just for her to hear. "You're my Bond girl. You're supposed to look adoring."

She relaxed in his arm, picking up the play, and grinned. "That makes you Bond."

"You never know." He tipped his head toward her.

Sunlight cut through the trees and caught her face. Her eyes sparkled. He reached down and brushed her cheek with the back of his finger. The strongest longing he ever remembered surged through him.

He dipped his head. Her eyes widened and lips parted, drawing him in. He was about a breath away when a group of loud individuals came up the path and she pulled back.

He felt her gasp just before he released her. There was

no missing now the blush that crept up her cheeks. He caught her hand to help her off the rock and back to the trail. Her fingers trembled slightly.

"Those were great shots," Paige exclaimed.

Thayne realized she'd handed Emma's camera off to someone else while she'd been taking pictures with his phone.

"Oh," the sound escaped Emma. She reached for her camera. "Thank you," she said to the middle-aged woman, who smiled back. "We better hurry back to the boat." She took off down the trail.

Paige arched an eyebrow as she handed over his phone.

"You're matchmaking," he accused.

She just shrugged. "I'm a pretty good judge of character. I like you. Emma is very reserved, make that extremely. I want her to find someone. Just don't disappoint me or I'll have to hunt you down," she threatened.

"You'll be in Bangkok," he pointed out.

"Won't matter." She eyed him a minute. "I've never seen Emma spark at meeting someone like she did with you. Don't hurt her."

Was it true? Thayne found he really wanted to believe it. He nodded. "Message received and for the record. I don't want to hurt her." He just hoped she really was what she appeared. Not that he planned on getting involved with her, he told himself.

They headed down the trail, emerging onto the beach where the boat was being loaded. Emma was in line, but what caught his attention was the man watching her from under the rock overhang.

Thayne had noticed the man on the other beach. He was too large to miss and even in his big, flowered swimsuit, he didn't seem to fit the tourist look. He was one of the reasons Thayne had held back on making the pickup.

The man had just been standing around. He'd raised his camera a couple times, but didn't seem to be taking pictures of anything on the island but people. Thayne thought one of the people was Emma.

Now he was sure. The man's attention was focused solely on her, and not in a way a man checks out a beautiful woman. The hair on the back of Thayne's neck stood up. This was a problem.

He fought back the swear word that wanted to slip free. If Emma wasn't involved any more than by accident, she was now. A simple pickup, right. Thayne brought up his phone and snapped two pictures of the overhang making sure the man was in clear focus, before he got in line to board.

For lunch they pulled up to a fishing village, which had a row of at least six open-sided buildings that were built on stilts over the water. Boats were docked and after the women covered over their swimsuits and the men put on shirts, the people from the tour were taken to their section where round tables were decked out with tablecloths and dishes. The chairs even had lace covers.

They sat down at a table and were joined by a couple from England, a young woman, about Paige and Emma's age from Russia, a man from France, and a teen age boy from China. They hardly had time to introduce themselves before the food started coming. First, was a whole cooked fish, then a couple vegetable dishes that were like a Pad Thai, rice, fish soup, fried shrimp and lastly French fries, which brought laughter to the Americans.

"Wow, look at all this," Emma said.

"What do you want to try?" Thayne asked.

She shrugged. "A little of everything."

Everyone took a portion and passed the food.

"So when did you move to San Diego?" Thayne glanced over at Emma.

"About six months ago. Driving was getting a bit much

for me."

"It's an expensive place to live on your own," he commented.

"Tell me about it. I've been renting a room from a co-worker at the hospital, before that I commuted from my parent's house in Laguna for almost a year."

"You lived at home?"

She shifted in her seat. "I moved back after college. My grandmother was living there at the time, and my parents needed the extra help taking care of her."

"That was nice of you."

She shrugged. "It was my grandma. She'd had a bad fall."

"You said you've been renting a room."

"She's getting married in a month, so he'll be moving in. She said I could stay for a while, until I could find something I wanted, but they need to be alone. I'm looking for something."

"Want, as in buy?"

"If I can afford to and it's a good deal. I wouldn't mind getting a place, even a fixer upper. I'm not afraid to work on it, and I know my father would help if I need it. I'm looking at the options."

"Where did you go to school?" he probed a little deeper while she was talking freely.

"I started locally at Saddleback and Irvine Community then went to Cal for grad."

"Any brothers and sisters?"

"One of each. Oldest is my sister. She's married and lives in Colorado and has two kids. My brother just graduated from dental school and bought into a practice in the Vegas area. He's married with one little girl. I'm the youngest. What about you?"

"One sister, who I see infrequently." Thayne couldn't believe he admitted the truth. He usually lied when asked.

"Why?"

He looked into her eyes and answered. "I don't get along with my brother-in-law. They don't have any kids. Kids would take her attention away from him."

"I get it. What about your parents?"

"They were killed in a car accident when I was in college." He glanced away then back when he felt her hand come down on his.

"I'm sorry."

He looked down at her hand. She drew it back as if realizing what she'd done.

"It's okay." He wanted her hand back, wanted her touch. "It was a long time ago."

"What do you think of the fish soup?" she asked changing the subject. "The lemon broth was kind of a surprise."

"I like it."

"This vegetable and noodles is real good." She reached up and put another scoop of it on her plate.

"I found a place on the beach last night I ought to take you to. You'll love it." He winced at what he was doing. He'd about asked her on a date. "Well, I think I'm done." Thayne pushed back. He could tell his abruptness startled her, but didn't let it stop his need to get away from her before he did anything else stupid. "If you'll excuse me, I'll catch you later."

He barely waited for an answer before he stood making his way through the tables back to where there were shells and other souvenirs for sale and the restrooms. Once out of sight, he continued through to the next seating area, then back where there was no way he could be seen. He pulled out his phone, activated it and hit dial. It was picked up on the second ring.

"Thayne, what's up?" Griff, the newest recruit said cheerfully for what would have been the middle of the night where he was.

"So they got you manning the front," Thayne said.

"Yeah, but all's quiet, so I'm getting in some quality gaming time."

Thayne shook his head. The guy was addicted to video games but he could also do anything with a computer. "I need you to do a check for me. Everything you can come up with. Sending you a picture. Name's Emma, no last. Works as a speech pathologist at a hospital in San Diego and an elementary school in the area. Graduated Cal a couple years ago."

"Okay, give me five or ten minutes and I'll send you a file."

Thayne shook his head but didn't doubt him. If anything was out there, Griff would find it, good or bad. He was almost afraid there would be nothing bad, which would be really bad. Because if Emma was just what she appeared, he was afraid he was in more trouble than he could handle.

"I'll be waiting." Thayne turned and caught sight of Emma, Paige, and the Russian girl looking at seashells in the souvenir area. He stayed back and watched. This time none of them seemed interested in buying anything.

He started to follow them when he caught sight of another familiar figure. Even at the distance, he had no problem recognizing the man who he'd seen on Bond Island on the boat dock. His dark hair and round face was far too large for the average Thai. Nor was he as tanned. In fact, he was a little sunburned. Once more the man's attention was focused on Emma.

Pulling back out of sight, Thayne raised his phone and snapped a couple pictures and sent them with the one of him and Emma to Griff with a message. "Any chance you can find out who this guy is? He's a little too interested." He pushed send.

Chapter Four

Thayne's instinct was to go to Emma, but he hung back and watched.

The women headed to the boat dock, still talking. Thayne glanced at the time. Six minutes had passed but it was time to go to the boat. He took a step in that direction and his phone vibrated. He looked at the message from Griff.

"Here's the file on Emma Anne Stephens. Pretty. I'll keep looking into her and see what I can find on the Big Boy. Get back to you when have more."

Thayne uploaded the file, but didn't take time to open it as he headed for the boat. He didn't see Big Boy again until he was about to climb on board. The man was in a small private boat moored one building over. Thayne shifted and leaned out as if getting a picture of the restaurant. Instead, he got a closer picture of Big Boy and the other two that were in the boat.

One looked like a Thai, probably the driver, but the other, though smaller, looked more lethal than the first. If Thayne didn't miss his guess, which he was pretty sure he didn't, Big Boy was a boxer, brawler. He was muscle, not brains, but the other, by the scar on his chin, was a knife fighter, smart and agile. Thayne didn't need to see a blade to know it was there. More than ever, Thayne didn't like it. He wished he had time to open the file to see if Emma checked out, but before he could the motors started up and the tour boat eased forward. Thayne knew he'd have to wait, but just as sure as he was that he'd pegged Big Boy and Blade right, he knew Emma was going to check out.

He pushed a hand back through his hair. Things were getting complicated, and he was afraid it was just the tip of the iceberg. Blowing out a breath as the boat pulled away from the dock, he watched the other boat follow. It didn't take long for it to fall behind, but Thayne knew it would be there on their tail. He made his way to the front of the boat as it picked up more speed.

He resigned himself to having to stay close to Emma. He tried to tell himself it was his responsibility, but when he saw her and his heart picked up a beat, he knew it wasn't the truth. Unable to wait, he opened the file on his phone to take a cursory look. It only took a second to get the gist that everything Emma had said and what he felt was true. Emma was the real thing, an incredibly sweet, warm woman that drew him in. He closed the file and headed toward her.

Emma didn't say anything when he sat down beside her. Thayne knew that by the abruptness in which he'd turned cold on her and left, he probably deserved it. He waited a second then started up the conversation. "Pretty interesting place."

She turned to look at him, a touch more closed off compared to what she'd seemed before. "Yes."

"It sure would be a different way of life." He tried again.

"Yes."

He studied her. "Is something wrong?"

A faint smile pushed its way to her lips. "No."

"Emma, I want to apologize at how abrupt I acted back there." He could tell he definitely surprised her. "I needed to take a step back and catch my breath."

That openly shocked her. Her lips parted but she was speechless.

"I don't want to come on too strong, but I find you very interesting."

"Oh." The sound finally slipped out of her.

He had the urge to kiss those lips. Talk about coming on too strong. "Anyway, I don't want you to worry. I did some thinking, and I was hoping we could enjoy the rest of the day together. Then, maybe at the end of the day, I could give you my phone number and when we get back to the states, you can decide, if you'd like, you can call me."

He could see her going over everything he said. They went over a bump and he caught her arm to steady her. She didn't pull back like he expected.

"Okay," she said slowly, and she bit the edge of her lip in a tempting little way.

"So, did you get souvenirs?" He changed the subject hoping to help her relax.

"No, I got a magnet on Bond Island. In fact," she unzipped the money wrist band and took the magnet out. She turned to her friend. "Paige, I'm going to put this in your backpack."

"Sure," her friend replied. "Will you put it in the cubby?" Paige handed the pack over.

Thayne watched Emma put the magnet into the small back pocket.

"Here, I'll do it." Thayne stood. "I have to get into mine."

Emma handed him the pack without hesitation. Thayne used the cubby door to block their views as he slipped out the magnet she bought and replace it with the one he had. Then he placed the magnet into a waterproof sleeve and put it into a pocket sewn into his trunks.

He returned to Emma and sat beside her as they went to the next couple islands. The last place was a long beach where they had an hour and a half to play in the water or lay on the beach and relax.

After, they walked up and down the length of the

beach while they talked about nothing specific. They returned to where Paige was laying on a towel. Emma stretched on her stomach beside Paige and closed her eyes while Thayne sat on the sand.

"Paige." Emma's voice was a low contended purr. "Will you put some more sunscreen on my back?"

"Sure." Paige rose up on her knees, picking up the tube.

Impulsively, Thayne put out his hand and to his surprise Paige actually handed over the tube then quietly rose and walked away to buy a drink from the peddlers on the beach. Thayne settled on Paige's towel and contemplated the expanse of tanned, satin smooth skin offered up to him before squeezing a line of sunscreen across it.

It wasn't the first time he'd ever put sunscreen on a woman in the line of work, but for some reason he was having trouble convincing himself it was work. It had been a longer time since he'd done it for his own pleasure. Five years since his wife died. And, they'd been married for almost two year. It had been seven years since he'd touched a woman who was not his wife, for the pure pleasure that he wanted to.

It hit him, how long it had been since he'd let himself live. Yeah, he went through the motions and convinced himself he was happy, and in a way he was, but there was a part of him that had shriveled and died with his wife. He stopped the thought, not wanting to go there any farther. That was in the past. So what did that make this – the future? No, still awareness radiated up his arms when he touched Emma's back.

He felt as much as heard her gasp. She started to pull up and turn on her side.

"Easy." He pressed his hand down, applying enough pressure to hold her there.

"Where's Paige?" There was a slight tremor in her

voice.

"She went to get a drink."

"But–"

"It's okay. I won't hurt you. Scouts honor." He held up his hand and pulled his fingers into the sign of the pledge.

She watched him over her shoulder. "You were a scout?"

"Yes. I'm an Eagle Scout."

"My brother was an Eagle Scout."

He repeated the scout oath to her then smiled. "I haven't thought of that in years."

She lowered herself back down, presenting her back to him. "Maybe you should get active in scouts again."

The thought actually didn't sound half-bad. "Maybe I should." He placed his hands on her back and began to rub. It quickly turned into more of a massage then putting on lotion. He was aware of every curve and play of her muscles. He memorized each spot that made her gasp or sigh.

He pressed down and slid his hands all the way up her back and over her shoulders and down again. She moaned with pleasure, and he repeated the action bringing his hands down her arms before shifting up and over her back.

"Oh," she groaned. "That feels wonderful."

He definitely wanted to agree.

"I was thinking about getting one of the massages you see advertised all around, but I don't think they could be better than this."

"Maybe I should charge three hundred baht."

"Too late, you should have negotiated first." She sounded slightly sleepy.

"Oh, but you're the one who is supposed to negotiate first. Otherwise, I can ask what I want."

"And, what do you want?" It came out followed with a sigh.

You. The thought hit him strong, but he held his tongue

because he was enjoying it as much as she was and didn't want to make her nervous. After a minute more, he decided he better stop before he gave into what he wanted to do and follow his hands with his mouth. Not answering, he stretched out on Paige's towel next to her.

A second passed and he thought she'd fallen asleep when she shifted. "Would you like me to put lotion on your back?"

He didn't think he could stand the thought of her hands on him and was prepared to say, "no need," but "yes, please," came out.

⊂ざ∾

Emma sat up and blinked a couple times. She felt totally relaxed and tingly at the same time. She picked up her lotion and squeezed some into her palm. It dawned on her the last man she'd put sunscreen on was her brother, before that maybe one of the guys in college.

She'd been used to doing it on the swim team, but that was just normal with friends, and none of them compared with Thayne. Oh, a lot had fine, well sculptured muscles, but his were – Emma wasn't quite sure how to explain them. Well, sculptured, fit, lean, definitely not bulky, firm but they were – more.

First, she spread lotion across his shoulders and down his back feeling the warm muscles rippling under her fingers. Emma liked the feel. On his left side, she noticed a small scar that was about an inch long. She traced over the area. He twitched under her administration and she smiled. An impulse to lean down and kiss the spot shocked her. She pulled back quickly.

Earlier, she'd noticed a scar on his chest just below his collar bone and one that etched across the top of his right bicep. They were proof of the active life he led, though it did confuse her how he'd gotten a scar on his back.

Of one thing she was sure, it was not because he was clumsy. Thayne moved with the smooth grace of a cougar.

The animal suited him, golden, lean and powerful.

Emma froze, halting her fanciful thoughts, realizing her actions had changed from putting lotion on him into caresses. "That should do it." She pulled her hands away, immediately missing the contact with him.

"I wish you wouldn't stop. That felt so good." His voice rumbled over her with huskiness.

"I..." She wasn't sure what to say, if she could even get words out. What did one say to a stranger that you'd been loving with your hands?

He rolled to the side and looked up at her. "What is it, Emma?"

"I..." She tried again without any more success. She bit the edge of her lip.

"You're not used to putting sunscreen on guys?" he asked helpfully.

"Not really. At least, not for a long time." She blushed.

"Is it just me?" He hit the point.

"I don't know you. We just met," she said then groaned, utterly embarrassed.

He stared at her and she felt trapped in his gaze. "Actually, you know more about me than most women of my acquaintance."

His words send a rush over her but reality stepped in. "Then I'd say few women know anything about you."

"That's true," he said honestly. "I tend to be a very private person. It's been a long time since I've been in any kind of a relationship."

"I find that hard to believe." She couldn't take her eyes off him.

"It's true." Honesty rang in the words.

"Why?" The question slipped out.

"Because it ended very badly last time."

"How bad?" Again, she couldn't seem to keep in the question but reached for his hand.

He looked down as if studying his fingers in hers. He

intertwined their fingers. "As bad as it can get." Pain echoed in the air.

"I'm sorry." Emma wished she could wipe away the question and his grief.

He shrugged. "It's been a long time."

"And you haven't tried another relationship since?" She really couldn't believe she asked that, knowing her own record.

"It didn't seem like a good idea. How about you? I get the feeling you aren't with anyone."

She knew it was fair of him to ask but she wasn't quite sure how to explain without feeling pathetic. "Paige says I'm too cautious."

"Nothing wrong with that."

"I'm … a little excessively so." She paused, but the words slipped out anyway. "I just don't want to be hurt. To know I made a bad decision again."

"I can understand that. So who made you so hesitant?" he asked gently.

"You're good at reading people." She tilted her head to the side.

"I have my moments."

She shook her head. "You'll think I'm silly."

"No."

"You will." She let out a breath. "Even I do." She looked away and back at him, took in and released another deep breath. "Would you believe it was in high school? It's so stupid."

"High school is a difficult time."

Emma knew the little laugh that escaped her was derisive. "Yes. Actually for the most part I handled it rather well."

"Except for this one."

"Yes."

"So what happened?" His thumb stroked over her knuckles.

"There was a guy. My first big crush. I had it bad. He was really popular, student body officer, captain of the swim team. Blond and built for a high school guy, and he seemed pretty nice. Not overly arrogant. To my surprise, he asked me out to one of the big dances. I was kind of nerdy, but I liked sports, especially volleyball. But, I wasn't tall enough for our coach. If you weren't at least five-ten, she wouldn't even look at you, no matter how good you were."

"Did they have enough girls that tall?"

She nodded. "All but one was over six feet. I practiced with them all the time, so I knew I could hold my own against them. It was just the coach's thing. And the funny thing, I was the same height she was."

"Okay. Back to the other, what happened at the dance?"

"It didn't happen."

"He cut out on you?" The utter disbelief in his voice and on his face was heartwarming.

"No, I called it off."

He waited, so she finally continued.

"Two days before the dance, I was outside waiting for Paige and my other friends for lunch. I was sitting on the ledge of the tiered area, kind of an amphitheater. There were bushes behind me then the tables. I was doing homework, a common occurrence. The group of guys he hung with came out and sat at the table on the other side of the bushes. They were talking about the dance and the girls. It was fast becoming a brag session. Then one of the guys said how this guy I was going with had already booked a hotel."

Thayne let out a low whistle but didn't say anything.

"Yeah. He had the nerve to tell them that he at least had enough style to give a girl her first time in a hotel room instead of in the car or on the beach. There was laughing. One of the guys asked if he was sure it would be my first time. This time he laughed and said they all knew it would, that 'I was one of the last of the good girls.' Another of the guys said, 'The pretty geek would fall at his feet,' and he answered, 'you got it'.

"I'm betting he didn't get it."

"Nope."

"I'm hoping you broke it off with him in front of everyone."

"Actually, I did. I was so upset, I burst. I told them how low and awful they were and called them a lot of disparaging names. A couple probably had no idea what they meant. I told him I wouldn't go to the dance or anywhere with him or any one of them ever. And I didn't. I didn't go out much in high school, just group stuff. My name was pretty much mud when it came to dating. At college, I got the opinion that the guys were just after the same kind of thing, the just having fun sex night."

"Yeah, I know the mentality. I promise I was never into that."

"Scout's honor?" she asked.

For the second time that day, he made the motion. "Scout's honor."

Emma forced a smile and leaned back on her towel.

Thayne followed the motion and met her eyes. She was mesmerizing. *What an idiot.* He'd love to find the guy and teach him a few things about hurting her, though the guy was probably married by now with kids.

His breath caught. He couldn't help wonder if that didn't mean, *could Emma, did that still mean, she was a virgin?* He shook his head but the possibility lingered in his mind. The problem was, it really did fit. He couldn't believe it.

He almost groaned aloud, barely catching the sound before it slipped free. She was too tempting, too innocent for her own good, and his. Not that he was into casual sex. He just had no place in his life for a woman like Emma. Not that he was even contemplating a relationship. The problem was those two guys watching her.

The curse for the melodramatic inclinations of the contact almost slipped from him. A simple pickup, once again the words came back to haunt him. He was going to have to keep an eye on Emma until he knew she was safe and that wasn't going to be until she was safely on a plane back home. Then he'd be out of her life, and she'd be out of his. He pushed away the touch of melancholy the thought brought.

Thayne cracked his eyelids to watch her. She was very pretty. Her soft pink lips were parted slightly in a sweet invitation he longed to accept. All it would take was rising up on an elbow and leaning over a couple inches. His finger ached to touch the strand of hair that had come free from her braid and ran down the side of her cheek, caressing her neck. He wanted to place his lips on that spot.

He closed his eyes trying to shut out the torment but the knowledge she lay beside him remained.

A spray of water shattered the peace that had settled over his body. A gasp beside him said Emma had experienced the same shock.

"Come on you two. The boat's leaving," Paige announced.

He opened his eyes in time to see the pixie trot away. Thayne wanted to close his eyes and wish the world away, mainly because that would mean his time with Emma was ending. This was their last stop, and he wasn't sure yet how he could wrangle more time.

The shyness was back in Emma as she stood and shook out her towel. When she failed to meet his gaze, he figured she was embarrassed about what she'd told him.

He wanted to slip his arms around her and draw her close and let her know it was all right. Instead, he picked up Paige's towel and copied her motions. They walked back to the boat in silence, being the last to arrive. Thayne wondered if she was as reluctant to have their time end as he was.

The ride back wasn't long. The tide was out, and the boat pulled up to a long dock instead of on the beach like it had that morning. He stepped out of the boat, turned and put out his hand. First, he helped out Paige then Emma. He had an urge to keep hold of her hand but released it. Still he stayed beside them as they walked back.

"That was so much fun," Paige said.

Thayne didn't miss Emma's glance at him. "It was wonderful."

He hoped that he was included in the wonderful part, but was afraid she was wishing she hadn't said anything about high school. He really hoped that bad memory hadn't tainted the day for her.

"It was the best time I've had in a long time." He caught her gaze and smiled. "So what was the favorite thing you saw?

"Oh, it was all spectacular." Before his eyes, excitement boiled up and poured out of Emma. "The way the, I don't know whether to call them islands or rock formations, thrust up out of the water, so beautiful. The beach, lunch, the cave, it was all amazing."

"What about you?" Paige directed her question to him.

His smile deepened. "I have fond memories of the beach, and there were definitely some highlights on James Bond Island." He looked directly at Emma, his gaze settling on her lips. There was no mistaking her knowing his time with her was the most special. He wondered what she would do if he wrapped her in his arms and kissed her.

Unfortunately, they reached the end of the pier. "I guess this is goodbye," he said to Paige. "Good luck in Bangkok." He turned to Emma. "It was nice meeting you. I hope to run into you in San Diego."

"Goodbye." Her eyes seemed to hold him. "It was nice meeting you." For a moment, Thayne thought she'd say something more, but she didn't.

"Bye, Thayne." Paige ended for them, and they disappeared into the crowd.

Thayne made his way to the tour organizer. It didn't take long to find which van was taking them and that there was an empty seat in it. Slipping the driver four-hundred baht was all it took to secure the seat and be dropped off after them. A few minutes later when the van was almost full, Thayne climbed into the front passenger seat next to the driver.

"Hey," Paige said, "what are you doing here?"

He looked back over his shoulder. "Hi, long time no see. They traded me because I was left off his list earlier but I'm more on this route and not as far out of the way for the other driver."

With that the driver started the van. They didn't get to talk much because they were toward the back of the van.

As they got out of the van he called their attention. "Emma, Paige, you're not far from my hotel. Maybe I'll see you on the beach."

"Maybe," Paige said, her lips twitched knowingly.

"Bye, again," he said directly to Emma.

"Bye." She smiled.

This time he felt the heat in it. *Man, she was beautiful.* He watched them disappear inside as the van pulled away. Thayne saw a hotel from a major chain a short ways down on the same beach and called Griff to make a reservation for him. That done he opened the file on Emma Anne Stephens and began to read.

 CRBO

"What a great day," Paige said as she flopped back onto her bed.

"Yes." Emma stretched out on the other. "Do you want the first shower? I'm exhausted."

"Really? After your nap on the beach?"

There was no missing the wicked tone in her friend's voice. "Paige!"

"Come on, you know you like him."

"Yeah, and I'll never see him again." The thought hurt for some odd reason. It wasn't like she'd had time to really fall for Thayne.

"You don't know that."

Emma shook her head. Paige was a pure romantic. "I'm leaving in three days. San Diego is a big city. There is just no way. I'll never see him again. Besides if I did, I kind of sabotaged any chance that he would be interested."

"Trust me. That man was interested."

"Not now."

Paige pushed up from the bed and looked over at her. "What did you do?"

Emma winced. "I told him about what happened in high school." Emma didn't have to wait long for Paige's reaction that she knew was coming.

"What! You didn't. Please tell me you didn't."

Paige looked aghast, and Emma could understand why. She couldn't believe she had. Inside she groaned. She'd never told anyone. Paige knew because she was there to see the blow up.

She groaned aloud. "I didn't mean to. It just kind of came out while we were talking."

She was so inept at dealing with men. Correction, just men she was interested in. Fortunately, there weren't many of those. With other men she was fine. She had a lot of male friends and colleagues, and she had no problem with those.

With Thayne, her emotions felt over-charged and all over the place. She had reacted so strongly to the man. She didn't know what to do. She could still feel his every touch on her body, from the first one that morning when he'd kept her from falling, to his putting sunscreen on her.

Paige was right. She really did like him. She liked talking to him, listening to him, the way he smiled, and just being by his side.

She wished she could see him again, but she didn't even know his last name, and he hadn't asked for hers. He had said he was going to give her his number, but after what she told him, it wasn't a surprise he hadn't.

She was pathetic. She sighed and tried to push down the longing. There would be no accidental meetings. Emma felt loss like she'd never had before.

෪

Thayne watched, ready to hop onto the small motorcycle he'd rented as the two women came out of the hotel. He pulled on the helmet as the taxi door was opened for them. Luckily, it wasn't hard to keep them in sight. They didn't go far, just down to the shopping area. The hardest thing was resisting the urge to join them.

They'd both showered and changed. Paige wore a pair of shorts and a v-neck T-shirt. Emma had on white pants that went to her calves and a bright pink shirt that scooped around her neck and was gathered tight at her waist with elastic so it added enough accent that he couldn't fail to notice her figure. The most glorious thing was her golden hair hanging free half-way down her back. In a sea of shorter, dark-haired people, she was a beacon, easy to spot.

She drew attention, which she seemed oblivious to, but there was no way she wouldn't. She was beautiful. Fortunately, there didn't seem anyone overly interested in them but the people trying to sell their goods. Thayne looked hard, especially for Big Boy and Blade, but with relief he didn't see them. Though, he doubted it would last that way no matter how much he wished.

The two shopped for about an hour before they stopped at a restaurant to eat. They were seated at a table right above the sidewalk. The open-air sides of the building made it easy to keep an eye on them so he ducked into a similar place across the street and ordered dinner, too.

A bus cut-off his view and when it passed, Thayne was greeted to the sight of three men in their early twenties and probably American, Australian or European, trying to make conversation with Emma and Paige. After a few minutes of obviously trying to persuade the women to join them, they finally gave up.

Thayne arched and rolled his shoulders to release the tension he hadn't realized he had. He wasn't sure how he'd handle it if the women went to one of the night clubs the area was famous for. To his relief, after they finished eating, they shopped a little more then headed back to their hotel.

After a half hour, he was pretty sure they were not coming back out, but he wasn't ready to chance it yet. Two hours later he finally accepted the fact and turned in his motorcycle. Settling into a chair on the beach he angled to give him view of the hotel lobby, he pulled out his phone.

This time Matt answered. "Thayne, what's going on?"

"The simple pickup developed a glitch."

Matt swore in his ear. "I was afraid from what Griff said that was the case. Though, I was hoping you'd just finally taken an interest in someone. Tell me about it."

"There just happened to be someone else from San Diego on the boat, and she just happened to stopped at the booth for a souvenir."

"Emma Anne Stephens. I don't like coincidences but I read her file and had Griff do a double check, even made some calls. She checks out," he affirmed.

"Figured," Thayne acknowledged.

"Did you get the chip?"

Thayne couldn't believe Matt even had to ask. The man must be upset. "Yes, it's on me now." Thinking about it made the area itch, and he had to resist the urge the rub where it was attached to his hip. "It's secure," he stressed. Even if anyone searched him it would look like a small scar on the side of his hip.

"Then everything's all right."

"I think we have a problem. The pickup place wasn't

clear. They made the Stephens woman."

"You're sure?"

"Yes. They watched her."

"Maybe it wasn't because of the chip." Thayne could hear the hope in his boss's voice. "She's a pretty woman. Over there, her looks would definitely stand out."

"True, but don't get your hopes up."

"What are you going to do?" There was an edge to Matt's voice.

"Keep an eye on her until she goes home. It's the day before my flight."

There was another swear word. "I was afraid you were going to say something like that."

"I'm not going to leave her hanging," he said firmly.

"I know. I wasn't suggesting it." There was a sigh over the line. "What do you need?"

"Hopefully, nothing. But, why don't you talk to our friends and see just how valuable this thing is. We're at a need to know, now. Depending on their answer, why don't you get some feelers out for a safe house just in case and get working on another ID for her if I have to pull her out of here?"

There was a second pause. "Agreed. I'll get back to you on that."

"Good." Thayne felt a touch of relief. He was afraid he'd have to do more coaxing. It worried him a little he didn't. That meant something was tingling Matt's instincts, too. "Has Griff found out anything about the guys yet?"

"No."

Right there Thayne knew one thing that was bothering Matt. If Griff couldn't find anything, that meant trouble. "I'll keep in touch," he said.

"Take care." The edge was deep in Matt's voice. He was concerned.

"Got it." Thayne disconnected the line.

Thayne stared at the well-lit lobby. There were a few

people coming in but no sign of anyone leaving. The breeze off the water stirred his hair. He stared out over the water. Clouds were building up and coming in. They were in for a night shower.

The moon cut through an opening in the clouds and reflected off the water. It was beautiful. He wished Emma was there to see it with him. He turned his attention back to the hotel. He waited another hour before he was certain Emma wouldn't be leaving before he returned to his hotel to get some sleep.

Thayne was back on the beach the next morning when Emma came out with Paige, carrying a duffle. He watched the two hug as the driver loaded the bag in the taxi. Paige settled in the car and Emma stepped back and waved. The car pulled away and, instead of going back inside, Emma crossed the street to the beach.

Thayne pulled back so she didn't see him but there was no worry as she turned the opposite direction. Emma slipped off her sandals, picked them up and walked down to the water's edge.

Her hair was held back in a simple ponytail, and she wore a white cover-up that came to the top of her thighs and set off the tanned skin. She looked at peace as she stared out over the waves rolling up to end just before reaching her. After a few minutes, she walked along the shore.

More than anything Thayne wanted to join her but held back thinking it might be too soon after Paige's leaving for an accidental meeting. He didn't want her to think he might be watching and frighten her, so he walked on the other side of the trees that ran between the street and the beach. They covered almost a mile before she turned and made her way back.

Once back in front of her hotel, she reached over her head and pulled off the cover-up. She had on the same swimsuit as the day before. Its familiarity did nothing to diminish the impact of seeing her in it. In fact, after his night's dreams, she was even more of a temptation. He'd awakened from a dream of following his hands over her body with kisses.

When she settled into a beach chair and pulled out her sunscreen, he almost lost the battle of remaining out of sight. Luckily, she made quick work of putting on sunscreen before she pulled a tablet out of her bag and settled back to read.

A longing to just sit beside her hit him again. Thayne fought it back down as he dropped into a chair of his own. It had never been so hard to keep an eye out for possible danger. His gaze kept returning to Emma and wanted to stay. He forced himself to watch for Big Boy, Blade or anyone else that looked like they might be watching her, besides him.

Mid-morning, an older man with a self-assured swagger, a chunky gold necklace and several gold rings on his fingers strolled down the beach and spied her. Getting a look of a kid in a candy shop, he headed her direction. Thayne stood and headed her way. He was about ten feet behind her chair when the man saw him and froze. He looked back at Emma then to him. With muscles already tense in his body, Thayne met his gaze straight on, challenging him. The man took a step back then wisely continued down the beach.

Unable to back away Thayne settled in a chair that was only two rows behind her. The woman needed a keeper Thayne thought an hour later when he sent a glare at another man that took notice of her.

To Thayne's relief, a few minutes later, he saw her begin to shut off her tablet. He rose quickly and moved over by the drink shack before she saw him.

Chapter Five

Emma felt lonely. It was an odd feeling for her. She was usually comfortable with her own company. She tried to tell herself it was because Paige had left and she was in a foreign place all by herself, but it wasn't working. She'd known the truth when she'd seen the two men start to approach her, the one very good looking, but she was relieved when they had pulled back and left because they were not the man she wanted to see.

The biggest clue to what bothered her though was the hero in her book, every time her mind tried to craft a picture of him, it came up with Thayne. It didn't make any sense. She'd only met the man once. True, she spent more time with him then she'd spent with any single man in the last month, maybe year but it seemed strange he would take over her thoughts.

What was it that made him stay with her? She could swear she felt his presence, that if she looked over her shoulder, he'd be there. She wished he was.

Emma walked through the lobby with the little pool with water lilies in it. A variety of orchids hung from the pillars. Outside the walkway was framed with plumeria trees.

She took the bridge over the pool then went down the flower-lined walk to her room. Pulling her keycard from her bag, she bumped it next to the sensor. When the green light blinked, she opened the door and froze at the sight before her.

Emma clamped her hand over her mouth to keep back the cry that wanted to escape. She turned and fled for the lobby. The warm smile of the pretty girl behind the desk who tipped her head in greeting didn't bring pleasure to her like it usually did.

"I need help." Emma burst out. "Someone broke into my room." She fought to hold down the panic.

Alarm replaced the smile on the woman's face, and she picked up the phone as the other woman stepped round the desk to her. The woman hardly reached her before the manager was there asking if she was all right. Everything slipped into a fog of the security guard meeting them and going to her room. Emma stood in the doorway while her room was investigated, then she was let inside to go over everything to see what was missing.

She shuddered at the sight. Clothes were strung everywhere, several pieces were torn. Her suitcase was a shredded mess on the floor. Fear hit her again sending icy spears to her heart.

She shivered but continued her inspection. Her bags of souvenirs were dumped on the floor. Mattresses were off the beds. The chair was tipped over. Everything was a shambles, but she couldn't find anything but a few souvenirs missing.

Whoever the intruder was had even managed to open the safe, but fortunately her passport, credit cards and travelers checks were still there. She didn't have much cash at the time and most of it had been with her, along with her camera and tablet.

Two hours passed filling out reports. Not as much of her clothes were destroyed as she first feared. The manager arranged for all her stuff to be laundered and moved her to a new room which he directed her to personally. After making another set of apologies the manager left.

Emma found herself left alone to get settled. The

problem was, she felt very unsettled and couldn't stand the thought of being cooped up in the room but wasn't sure she felt safe going out either. Dropping onto the bed, Emma wrapped her arms around herself. Her body started to tremble then shake violently as tears slipped free.

Emma only gave herself a minute to cry before she pulled herself back together and wiped her eyes. She was not going to let this beat her. Crying didn't solve anything, and she hadn't lost much.

She was in a beautiful place and she was not going to let one stupid act destroy her time there. Still, there were things she had to face first. Number one, she needed a new suitcase.

Back on her feet, she paused long enough to wash her face before heading out. Her courage waned on the hotel steps. More than anything she wanted to return to her room, but even the suite they'd moved her into didn't feel safe – which was foolish. It was a random act of theft. The odds were against it happening again. Emma kept repeating the thought, but it just wouldn't sink in.

Emma forced herself to take a couple steps forward and had to admonish herself again as tears once more rose. She swiped away one that escaped. This was not helping her accomplish anything. She needed to go shopping. She needed – Thayne's name came to her mind along with his image. More than anything, she wished he was there.

⚬₰

Thayne saw Emma the moment she stepped out of the hotel and immediately became alarmed. She froze on the steps. There was an uncertain, vulnerability about her that pulled at him. She looked lost.

Dodging a couple of cars, he headed across the street, making it to the other side before he was even aware of his actions. Still, he didn't slow as he strode up the drive.

Her hand trembled over her lips when he reached her, and her eyes were luminescent with unshed tears.

"Emma?" he said softly but she jerked and spun, a small squeak escaped her. Her eyes locked on him. She blinked. After a second, she relaxed almost to the point of going limp.

"What's wrong?" He caught her hand.

She stared at his hand on hers a moment then raised her eyes to his. "You're here." The words came out as a whisper, as if she couldn't believe it was real, then her fingers tightened on his.

Panic surged in him. "What happened?" He caught her other hand.

"Some ... someone broke into my room." Her chin trembled.

"What?" He pulled her into his arms not giving her time to answer. She pressed her face into his neck. He felt her take a couple ragged breaths and wrapped his arms around her, pressing her tight.

Fury built in him but he tamped it down. He had to keep it together. He buried a hand into her silky hair at the base of her neck and eased her head back. "Are you all right?" The words hurt to ask. He picked up no evidence of assault. Still, it felt like bands constricted on his chest until she nodded.

"I was on the beach." Her words trembled, but she seemed more in control. She lowered her head back to his chest and took a shaky breath. When she raised her head, she gave a shaky smile. "Sorry."

He didn't release her. "Don't be." He brought one hand up to cup her cheek, stroking his thumb across it to wipe away the last of the moisture. "Tell me what happened."

He drew her over to a stone bench, keeping her tucked to his side.

She took another deep breath to steady herself. "Paige left. I took a walk on the beach then sat and read for a while." Her fingers intertwined with his.

"I went back to my room and opened the door." Her

breath caught again. "Everything was a mess."

"You didn't go in?" Fear hit him again.

"No, I ran to the front desk."

Relief surged over him. "Good."

"Did they call the police?"

She shook her head. "I don't know. The manager and security man took charge of filling out the report and moved me to a new room."

"Good."

"It doesn't look like whoever broke in took anything but shredded my suitcase."

The chill was back and anger seethed. It was his fault. He'd hoped....

"Thank you." Her words cut through his self-recrimination. "I needed someone right now."

He stroked her chin again. "Are you sure you're all right?"

She managed a weak smile. "Yes. As I said, I wasn't there and they didn't take much. The main thing is I need to replace my suitcase." She took another deep breath and straightened. "That's where I'm headed."

"Would you like me to go with you?"

She looked totally surprised at his offer, then relieved, but shook her head. "You don't need to waste your time—" She started but he cut her off with a finger against her lips.

"Emma, would you like me to go with you?" he repeated slowly.

"Would you?" she asked this time.

"Yes."

The smile she gave him was like he'd just slain a dragon for her.

"I don't know where to go."

"Come on." He kept her hand in his and turned to hail a cab with the other.

The shopping area was swarming with people.

"I was down in this area last night with Paige. I didn't

pay any attention to who had suitcases," she said as they stepped out of the cab.

"That's all right. We'll just wander. We're apt to find some. Until then, we just relax and enjoy." He again caught her hand.

She didn't say anything but smiled at him.

They walked by a place that had bright-colored pants flooding out on the walk. A woman called at them to look.

"Would you like a pair?" he asked.

"I thought about it, but can't see myself wearing them back home. Though the wrap skirts I keep seeing are tempting."

"Then let's get one." He drew her to the next shop that had the skirts.

"I really don't need one. The hotel is having my clothes cleaned."

He picked up her slight shiver.

"That's not the point. The point is that it's fun. So which color do you like?"

"I need to go change some travelers checks first."

"No need. My treat. I kind of like this." He picked up one that had a royal blue thread in it and held it up to her. "Do you like it?"

She laughed. "Yes." They looked at several others but she kept coming back to the royal blue. Thayne finally turned to the woman and started to negotiate the price.

"I'm not even sure it will fit," Emma said.

"Oh fit all sizes. You easy fit," the woman said hurriedly, opening the skirt to show how it wrapped around.

They agreed on the price and Thayne handed over the money and took the bag. "What next?" he asked.

"You really didn't need to do that. I still have money. It was in my bag with me."

"It's okay. I wanted you to have something to remember me by."

"I don't think that will be a problem." The words seem to slip from her and she blushed.

"Good." On impulse he leaned down and brushed her lips with his.

She looked surprised but didn't pull back. "I … ah, really need to change my traveler's checks. You can't keep buying me things."

"It wasn't that much," he said, but at the look she gave him he conceded. "Okay, there's a bank down the street."

They shopped their way there, buying her a cloth purse with elephants on it that matched the color of her skirt. Emma got a couple scarves and fans and other gifts. When she picked up a magnet, he felt a lurch inside him.

"I thought you already bought one?" He touched her arm.

"I did, but I must've lost it, or it was in the bag that whoever broke in took; because I couldn't find it when I picked up everything."

She sounded more matter-of-fact now about the break in, but he felt another wash of concern.

"Really? I can't see a thief taking something like that."

"That's why I think I must've lost it."

"What else was taken?" He didn't want to upset her again but had to ask, needing to know if it might have been random and he was overreacting.

"Not much. It was more like a search. I really didn't have much there. No expensive jewelry or money. I was kind of surprised, but grateful, he didn't take my credit card or passport. The main thing I lost was my suitcase. The security guard figured he either was searching it real well or he got mad because he couldn't find anything."

"And he tore your suitcase apart?"

"Yes."

Thayne scanned the area as he had been doing all along. He took hold of her arm just above the elbow as they walked.

They finally reached the bank. It took about twenty minutes to change her money then they decided to eat before going farther. The small Thai place they went into was similar to the ones they each ate at the night before.

"I've found I really like the Thai food, though, not too spicy."

"I like the spicy," he said. "Bring it on."

He smiled and she smiled back.

They shared their dinners with each other. When they stepped back down on the street Emma looked at the sky. "It looks like the clouds are moving in."

Thayne glanced up. "Yeah, we're supposed to have an afternoon shower. Maybe we better find your suitcase and get back."

A couple shops down they found bags and suitcases. "See something you like?"

Emma went into the shop.

Thayne stayed back on the sidewalk, taking the time while she was totally distracted to pull out his phone. Max answered again.

"I'm surprised you're there," Thayne said in way of greeting.

"Working on another problem. How's it going?"

"It got worse. Her room was broken into and searched."

Max swore.

"Yeah, I need that safe house."

"Working on it. Should have it set in a couple hours. You need to get home."

"My plane's in three days. I want her on it with me."

"Thayne—"

"I mean it." Thayne cut him off. "I'm not leaving her."

"All right. I agree, but are you sure it's best to keep her with you?"

"Yes, that's the way it stays." He looked at Emma. He always wanted her with him.

"I'm working on it. Get back to me in a couple hours. Who needs sleep anyway?"

Thayne hung up on the comment. Sliding his phone back into his pocket, he stepped into the shop going to her. "Find anything you like?"

She glanced at him. "I'm thinking of this one."

He lifted it up. The zippers were good and it had heavy duty wheels. "Looks good," he said.

"You have phone service?"

"I have a local sim card." He didn't try to deny it.

"That's right. You said you have business here. I'm not causing a problem am I?" She looked concerned.

"No." He lied easily, but, it was also the truth. The problem was not her fault.

"Am I keeping you from work?" she asked as if she sensed something was not quite right.

"Nope, I don't have anything for two more days. You're a blessing, giving me something to do instead of sitting around by myself. I'd much rather pass the time with you."

She eyed him a second as if trying to decide if he was telling the truth. She must've accepted it, she smiled. "I'm glad you're here. You've made my day much better."

"Good, but I'm not done yet. Now let's get your suitcase." He let her do the negotiating for the suitcase. He'd noticed earlier she had gotten into the process, which he'd had to agree was a lot of fun.

When done, she turned back to him. "Nice. Shall we put all this stuff in there?"

They loaded the bag.

Thayne was about to hail a cab when he noticed a shop across the street. "One more thing, come on." He grabbed the handle of the suitcase in one hand then took her hand with his other, pulling her across the street.

"What's this?"

"You'll see."

She went with him but at the shop with women's swimwear, she paused instead of going in. "Thayne, I don't need a new suit. Mine wasn't damaged."

"That's good to know, but you said your stuff was being laundered. And for what I'm thinking of this afternoon, you'll need a suit."

"What are you planning?"

"Trust me. You'll enjoy it."

"But it's going to rain." She tilted her head up to the sky.

"No problem. I'm thinking that one." He pointed to the suit on the top row. Her eyes followed the motion of his hand to the one piece suit similar to the one she wore the day before. This one had an oriental flare, black and white floral print with a row of knotted type catches going down the front. Halter neck with her back and sides bare. He had no problem picturing her in it.

"Oh." The sound came from her.

"I take it that means you like it."

"I don't really need it." The words were slow coming out for her.

"But you like it," he pressed.

"It's pretty," she admitted. "But, I don't even know if they have one that would fit me." She was already stepping in.

Thayne was about to follow her when he caught sight of a man crossing the street. The man had a smooth, gliding stride on the balls of his feet, for quick light movements. Even with the ball cap and sunglasses, Thayne didn't have any problem recognizing him from the way he moved.

Blade was a lot craftier and didn't stand out as much as his big friend. Thayne knew it was only that he'd been looking for them that he noticed the man. It worried him slightly that he hadn't picked Blade up before now.

Thayne glanced back at Emma. She was holding the swimsuit and talking to the shopkeeper. As much as he wanted to watch her, he looked back at the man who'd settled into a shop a ways down.

Trying to conceal his movements, Thayne looked around for Big Boy but couldn't find him anywhere. Thayne figured that meant one of two things. Either the Blade was on his own, or Big Boy was waiting in a car somewhere, which was most likely.

"What do you think?" Emma held it up.

He looked back at her. "I already told you I like it. It will look great on you."

"I also have this cover to match." The shopkeeper held up a white, light-weight cover that had a mandarin type collar and would come to the top of Emma's thighs.

"Perfect," he said, meaning it. He stepped toward them ready to start bargaining but Emma beat him there.

"Nope, I'll get it, if I like the price," she added, turning to the woman and started the debate.

Thayne wanted to tell her not to worry about the price because he wanted to see her in it, but she was having too much fun. For a minute, he actually thought Emma was going to walk away from it but they met at a price.

While Emma paid for the swimsuit and cover, he located Blade again. The man had moved up a booth and was in debate with the shopkeeper. Thayne guessed that as soon as they moved, Blade would drop the item and the shopkeeper wouldn't get his sale, but then Blade took out some money and handed it to the guy. Thayne caught a flash of something silver as Blade slid something into his pocket.

Thayne shifted out a little farther to see past the scarves cutting off his view to what the man was selling. Thayne couldn't see what was in the case by the man, but the katana type sword on the wall let Thayne guess – knives.

Thayne saw Blade's attention shift back toward them. He turned back to Emma. She was putting the swimsuit and cover in the suitcase.

"If I buy much more, I might have to buy another suitcase." She smiled up at him.

"Well, we know where to come." He smiled back. "Let's walk down this way." He again took the suitcase from her and headed away from Blade.

"Did you want something?"

"I thought maybe I'd see about getting a T-shirt and a cap while I was here."

"Okay." She fell into step with him.

Thayne was aware of every movement of Emma beside him. He was also aware of the man watching them. Blade stayed with them down the street. They passed several shops before Thayne stopped in one, getting Emma to help him pick out a shirt and a hat while he watched Blade and tried to find Big Boy. It bothered him that he couldn't find the large man. Thayne added a pair of shorts to his purchase, and there was still no sight of him.

He didn't think about asking before putting his stuff in Emma's suitcase. He just did it automatically, but noticed she didn't comment about it.

"Ready to head back?" he asked.

"Yes, I got a lot more than I planned on buying." She laughed.

"But you'll look great in all of it." He couldn't resist brushing a finger across her cheek.

She blushed lightly then shrugged. "If it fits."

"Let's go find out." Thayne held out a hand and a car pulled up as if by magic.

Thayne gave the hotel name and a price. When the man agreed, Thayne had him open the trunk. Thayne just lowered the suitcase in when the sound of a motorcycle and angry shots reached him.

He glanced over his shoulder to see a motorcycle cut up onto the sidewalk. He didn't recognize the two men on it but the course was clear. Emma!

Chapter Six

Thayne's focus shifted to Emma. Drawn by the commotion she turned toward the motorcycle bearing down on her. She tried to pull back but with all the stuff from the shop behind her, there wasn't any place to go.

Thayne leapt the five feet separating them, wrapped his arms around her, and pressed her into the mass of dresses and skirts hanging down the wall. He had no time to prepare as the edge of the handle bars struck his back. He sucked in a breath and jerked tighter into Emma.

She cried out, but her face was pressed into his chest so not much sound escaped. Thayne felt hands brush over him. One caught his side threatening to rip him away. He thrust his elbow back, contacting with flesh and was released, then he was free.

A second later, the roar died away. The motorcycle was gone.

Relief swamped his body. He couldn't bring himself to open his arms. He could feel Emma's breath stir against his neck where her face was pressed. Her delicate hands clung to his shoulders with surprising strength.

Noise grew around them again, but this time it was the chatter of people asking if they were all right. Thayne eased back.

"Are you all right?" Emma asked the question foremost on his mind before he could. She touched his face. Concern showed bright in her eyes as she looked him over.

"I'm fine." He caught her hand and pressed it to his cheek. "Are you all right?" Thayne studied her then wrapped his fingers around hers and brought them to his lips.

She nodded. "Thanks to you. It would've hit me."

"Probably after your purse. Do you still have it?"

"Yes, but the bike hit you?"

"I'm okay, just a glancing blow when the man reached for your bag." He brushed her concern away.

"Are you sure?" She didn't look convinced.

"Yes, I've had harder hits playing football with my friends." He kissed her fingers again then eased back a little.

"They didn't get your wallet?"

Her question had him checking just to be certain, but it was still in the front Velcro pocket where he kept it. "I've got it."

He finally became aware of the Taxi driver and shopkeeper asking again if they were all right. He stepped back from Emma but slid his arm around her, keeping her tucked into his side. His heart lurched when he felt her hand come up to rest on his chest.

"We're fine," Thayne assured them, noticing that people were starting to pick up stuff that had been knocked over. "Can you take us to the hotel now?" he asked the driver.

The man nodded, obviously shaken, but willing to help.

"You don't want to wait for the police?" Emma asked.

"There's nothing they can do. Nothing was stolen. It would probably be written off as someone being reckless," Thayne answered.

"But they hit you."

"I'm fine, Emma." He urged her into the taxi.

She slid over as he got in, but she stopped in the middle of the seat, her hands again going to him. She touched his side and ran her hand over his chest but her attention was focused on his face. "Are you sure you're all right?"

"Yes." He slid his arms around her and with just a slight amount of pressure she leaned into him and rested her head on his shoulder. The taxi started forward. He ran his hand up and down her arm a couple times then looked down at her. She tilted her face up to him in a silent offering he couldn't stop from taking any more than he could stop his next breath.

Fire filled him at the first touch of her mouth against his. A burning heat of passion grew as he let his lips linger. Just the taste of her ignited his soul, thawing a part of him that he'd thought had been frozen forever.

He buried his hand in her hair and held her tight as he savored and return the fervor he found. She was life, and she was his. The thoughts pounded in his head with each beat of his heart.

With a blare of a horn they were jerked to the side and thrown against the door as the car swerved, bringing him back to his senses. Emma eyes were closed, her lips parted, full and rosy from his. She was delicate. An innocent offering he wanted to accept.

He started to lower his head again but another blare of a horn snapped him back to reality. He instead pressed his lips to her cheek in a light brush. Her eyelids fluttered open. She smiled up then blushed.

He smiled back feeling happier than he had for years, if not ever. She laid her head on his shoulder. Silent, they remained cuddled together all the way back to the hotel and up to her room.

Thayne reached for her arm when she opened the door. "Let me check it out first."

He could tell he had surprised her, but she remained in the doorway while he went in. It only took him a moment to search.

"You really didn't think anyone would be there did you?" she asked as he walked back toward her.

"No, but it doesn't hurt to be careful."

"I can't believe this. We had no problems at all. This was one of the best vacations I've ever had."

"Well, don't let this ruin the memories for you. I think it's just one of those things." He stopped in front of her.

"I know. If I was really superstitious I'd be worried. They say trouble comes in threes. This has been two. What else could happen?"

Thayne didn't want to think of the possibilities. "I wouldn't worry about it. In fact, if you remember earlier, I mentioned I have something to take your mind off what happened. I think it will still be just the thing. So why don't you put your new swimsuit on, and I'll run and change into my suit and be right back."

"It's going to rain," she pointed out again but gave a little laugh.

"It won't matter. Now, don't open the door for anyone else." He leaned down and pressed a kiss to her lips, stepped back, and shut the door.

⋐⋑

Emma stared at the door a full minute before she could move. Shaking her head, she turned back to her room. She wondered what he was thinking, then placed a finger to her lips and wondered what she was.

Her lips still tingled from his kiss. She hardly knew the man, but it didn't seem to matter. In her heart, Emma felt like she had been waiting for him forever, and if that wasn't corny, stupid, and setting herself up for a big hurt, she didn't know what was. Still, she couldn't make herself pull away from him because when she was with him – it felt so right.

Emma went to the suitcase he'd left on her bed when he'd looked around her room and unzipped it. Taking out the swimsuit, she held it up and after a second headed into the bathroom to change.

Emma had to admit the swimsuit looked even better on than she even hoped. The fit was great, and she liked the mandarin flare of it. The high collared wrap was a perfect accent to it. Emma braided her hair, then wrapped it around her head and fastened it into place with an enameled hairpin she'd bought when shopping earlier with Paige. She was ready when the knock sounded at her door.

Thayne's words came back to her just as she was about to open it. "Who is it?"

"Thayne."

Her heart jumped at just his name as she opened the door.

"I … wow." He let his gaze run over her in open appreciation. "You are gorgeous."

"You like?" Emma felt a blush sweep into her cheeks. She'd been doing it a lot since she'd met him. She had never really worried overly about her looks but, for some reason, what he thought meant a lot to her.

"I like."

"You haven't even seen the swimsuit yet."

"Be still my heart." He placed a hand over his chest.

Emma laughed.

"You ready to go?"

"Yes. I see you came prepared." She motioned to the large umbrella he held in his free hand like a cane. She picked up her bag and followed him out.

"Be prepared, scout motto," he said as she locked and checked the door.

"Right. So, where are we going?"

"You'll see." He led her through the hotel and out onto the beach. Once on the sand, they both removed their shoes and went barefoot walking so only the occasional wave reached them. Clouds rolled over head, and a breeze came off the water helping to cool some of the ever present-heat.

They'd gone about a quarter mile when Thayne halted.

"Here we are."

"Here?" Emma looked around. The only thing she saw beside water and sand was a few little huts selling things and a row of cabanas where women were giving massages. It hit her then what he planned.

"You said you haven't had one," he said, confirming her guess.

She bit her lip, feeling a wave of anticipation. A drop of rain landed on her cheek dampening it. "What about the rain?" Emma glanced up, knowing any second the sky was about to let loose.

"We'll be under the cabana, out of it." He pulled her forward. "Come on."

She went with him. They broke into a run when the rain started to really come down.

A few minutes later, Emma sighed in pleasure and got lost in the sound of the rain pounding a soothing rhythm on the roof overhead and the feel of strong hands working their way up her leg. She figured the only thing that could have made it better was if they were Thayne's hands.

Emma smiled remembering his reaction when she'd removed the cover-up. His eyes had gone wide and a whistle had escaped him. She had felt the same when he'd pulled his shirt off. Yeah, she'd seen his chest the day before, but it didn't lessen the impact. He had a nice, well-toned chest.

Emma couldn't believe she was lying on the beach next to one of the best looking guys she'd ever seen with rain coming down around them. No one who knew her would ever believe it. Well, okay Paige would because she'd seen him and was always telling her she was selling herself short when it came to men. Paige always told her that the reason she couldn't find a man that she could fall in love with was because the men she thought she deserved bored her.

Emma opened her eyes and looked over at Thayne. He

didn't bore her. He sent up sparks in every level of her being – intellectual, physical and emotional.

She wondered when he'd look at her if he could just how plain and ordinarily blah she was? The thought brought a stab of pain. She knew it was foolish, but wished her time with him would never end. She wanted to stay forever in her own little paradise. At least, that was what it felt like when he was there.

Was it possible to fall in love in two days? It was probably just the wishful thinking of her inexperienced, romantic heart.

Why did he have to feel so right to her? If he didn't, maybe she would have a chance not to get her heart broken, because for once, she wanted to risk her heart. The only problem was – she felt like he was hiding something from her.

Emma didn't understand him that was for sure. At times, she felt a strong longing in him that shouted he just wanted to be near her. It was a heady feeling, and one Emma could understand because she felt the same way about him. But then, there'd been a few times when she'd felt him pull back, like he didn't want to be around her.

Those times had hurt, which was foolish because she'd just met him. She shouldn't have an emotional link to him. Link. The word hit her. It was how she felt, that they had a link, or maybe bond was a better word.

"Has anyone told you lately how beautiful you are?" His words caught her by surprise. Emma found herself looking into Thayne's clear blue eyes.

Pleasure filled her. "I think you just did and thank you."

"Do you like this?"

"It's heavenly. The only problem is I'll always be dreaming of another." She sighed.

"There are places in the states."

"I know. I have friends that go get massages. I just

could never justify doing it. I may have to change that, save up and splurge."

"Or you could always find a friend that gives a good massage and trade off. I think I could give a decent one."

Her breath caught. Was he saying he wanted to see her in the future? Emma tried to get the nerve to ask but was too afraid she'd read him wrong.

He reached over the space separating them and took her hand. His eyes seemed to burn as he looked at her. "It will be all right, Emma." His promise was definite.

She couldn't hold the need to know back. "Do you want to ...?" The words petered off at the intensity in his eyes.

"See you? Yes."

Emma wasn't sure if she could get a sound past her thundering heart, then a yelp escaped her as the woman giving the massage pressed her thumb into her foot.

Thayne laughed then groaned as he received similar treatment.

Please, please don't let him be a lie. Her heart screamed, her mind echoed. The image of him taking advantage of her didn't fit. Thayne was the hero type. She remembered the feel of him sheltering her with his body from the motorcycle. That was the real Thayne.

She glanced at his back. The proof was there on the side of his ribs. "You were hurt," she said, feeling a wave of concern.

"It's okay."

"You have quite a bruise."

"I'd rather it be on me than you."

She didn't want it on him either. The thought must've shown on her face.

"I'm all right, Emma." He stroked his thumb over the back of her hand. "Relax and enjoy."

"I am." She closed her eyes and let herself drift with pleasure, all the bad things of the day forgotten.

Emma's body felt totally fluid when the massage ended forty minutes later. The rain had eased from a down pour to just a sprinkle. Thayne opened the umbrella and wrapped an arm around her tucking her against his body as they started out onto the beach.

The world had the fresh after a rain smell and under that she picked up the fragrance of lemongrass oil from their massages. She sighed.

"Would you like to walk on the beach for an hour before we go shower and change for dinner?" Thayne asked.

"That sounds wonderful, if that means we're going to have dinner together?" Emma got up her nerve to ask.

"I was hoping you'd like to have dinner with me."

"I would love to." A thrill tingled all the way to her fingertips.

"Good." He smiled down at her then pulled her to a beach-side hut that sold jewelry. "What do you like?"

She laughed. "You've already bought me enough today. You don't have to get me anything else."

"These aren't very much, and they need to make a living."

He was right. The bracelets were less than a dollar.

"This one." She picked out one with little disks that looked like tiny ancient coins. "And I'd like to get a couple others to take home."

"Go ahead." He took the one she'd chosen and fiddled with it while she picked three more, then he negotiated the price and handed over the money. "Let's see your wrist." He wrapped it around and slid the knot through the loop fastener then tied a knot beside, so it couldn't come off. Emma almost objected, afraid she might have to cut it to get it off, but it was already done.

೮೩෨

The rain had moved on, and the evening was beautiful. Thayne stared across the table at Emma. She looked glorious. The lowering sun set fire to the sky and lit her up with flames of warmth. Her hair shimmered down her back in waves of gold. One side was pulled behind her ear, held back by a plumeria blossom, which he'd picked and tucked there on their way down.

The long straight skirt which they'd purchased earlier was a perfect accent to her long lean body. She was easily the most beautiful woman at the restaurant and a major contrast to the pretty, petite Thai women with their black hair and almond skin. He felt like a giant around them. He felt perfect with Emma. He liked the way she'd fit under his arm when they'd walked on the beach earlier and on the way down to the restaurant.

Waves crashed high on the sand only a few feet from their table.

She looked out over the water and smiled. "I love this. It's so beautiful."

"It doesn't get much better," he agreed.

"No, it doesn't. This is one of the things I will miss when I go home." She sighed.

"You know there are restaurants on the beaches there," he pointed out.

"I know, but this has been like a dream."

"Being in a tropical paradise can make you feel that way." He reached over laying his hand on hers. He found he really like to do that. Funny, he couldn't remember ever having this need to just touch a person.

"Yes. I want to thank you."

"For what?"

"For what you did today."

"Spending a day with a beautiful woman? My pleasure."

Emma beamed at his compliment.

Thayne drank her in. *Didn't the men in her life know something amazing when they saw it?*

"Thank you, but I think it was more in the line of a

hysterical, troublesome woman." One corner of her lip tilted up.

"I wouldn't call you hysterical. I thought you handled it rather well."

"You missed my crying session."

He traced a finger over the inside of her wrist, drawing out a small shiver from her. "As I said, you handled it quite well. And, I don't think I'd call you troublesome."

"You have the bruise to prove it. Remember? I saw it when we were having our massages."

"Oh, checking out my body, were you?" He got the blush he was after.

"I…" She paused and looked at him.

He could see her steadying her nerves, but she looked him straight in the eye.

"I won't deny I checked you out. I knew you got hit, and I wanted to be sure you were okay."

Thayne wasn't prepared for the disappointment he felt, that it had only been to see if he was okay. Was she only with him because he was the only person that she knew there – security thing? He'd been fooling himself that she was as interested as he was.

She drew in a breath, fiddling with her napkin. "Besides, I'm sure you know you have a nice body to look at." The words were said so quietly he almost missed them, but they were a balm to his ego.

He turned her hand over and interlocked their fingers. "I have good genetics. It just takes a little exercise to keep in shape. Are you an exercise junkie?" He thought of her toned body.

"No, but I enjoy swimming, walking and maybe a little jogging."

"Speaking of which, how about a stroll in the moonlight on the beach after we're finished here?"

"Yes."

Her whispered answer carried quite an impact. It was

all he could do to concentrate on finishing his dinner.

"Is it too spicy?" She looked at his food.

"No, not at all. Would you like a taste?" He held a forkful out to her.

She leaned forward and accepted it. "Mmm, not bad, a little hot for me. I'm so going to have to learn how to cook Thai food."

"You won't get any complaints from me," he answered with wink. When pleasure showed on her face, he was glad he did but he was going to have to get his head back in line. He was supposed to be keeping an eye on her to protect her, not fall in love with her.

"Thayne, is something wrong?"

Her question surprised him. She was too in tune with him. "No." He needed to talk to her. He just didn't want to ruin their time together. She deserved a nice evening and so did he.

For once, he wanted a nice evening with a woman that interested him. He wanted a minute just to feel like a normal man on a normal date, but he couldn't put off the discussion they needed to have much longer. He didn't feel safe with her being alone tonight at the hotel. He needed to get her to a safe house.

He glanced up and down the beach. It looked clear. He didn't know how he was going to explain everything.

A vision of his wife came to his mind and surprisingly, it didn't bring the old pain with it. Beth had known he worked for the government, but she thought he was an engineering troubleshooter. She'd trusted him.

Emma trusted him. He didn't want to ruin that trust. He really didn't want her to think the only interest he had in her was because of his job. He could still see the pain that idiot boy's betrayal caused her. His stomach tightened at the thought. He didn't want to cause her pain. He was no good for women, especially sweet, beautiful women like Emma.

Thayne made up his mind. He had to tell her now. "Would you like some dessert?" The words came out of his mouth instead.

She started to shake her head before he finished. "No. That was wonderful."

"Ready to go then?"

She nodded. "Just let me go freshen up first."

Not wanting her out of his sight his instinct was to say no but held his tongue as she stood and walked to the back of the restaurant. He waved the waitress over and asked for the check and handed over the money. He tried to wait patiently. Finally, after he twisted the napkin into a ball, he tossed it onto the table and rose. A movement caught his attention, Thayne shifted his gaze to the side of the restaurant.

Two forms moved in the shadows, slipping from the next restaurant over into the back of theirs. The big bull of a man was once again easy to make out where his companion might have disappeared into the shadows if Thayne hadn't been looking for him. Thayne quickened his pace but forced himself not to run and draw attention.

A slight squeal sounded just as he reached the bend to the back room. Thayne slipped around the corner. It opened into a concrete room lined with large water tanks filled with lobsters, squid, and fish, all waiting to be prepared. His focus skipped over them to the back of room where it opened into the alley and Emma was struggling against the two men.

Chapter Seven

Anger flared through Thayne at the sight of Big Boy's meaty palm clamped over Emma's mouth. He pressed his emotion down, and tried to ignore the terror in her eyes. Emma was not going easy. He felt a stab of pride. She thrashed her head back and forth, squirmed and kicked, but with her feet dangling a couple inches off the ground, she couldn't get enough leverage to free herself or do much damage to her captor.

Thayne had no restraint. Silently, he moved toward the men, picking the leaner man first. Whether it was the sound of a scuff on the floor or just instinct that warned the man, he spun. Thayne's nickname for the man held true as a knife appeared in the man's hand.

Blade swung at him. Thayne was ready for it. Sidestepping, Thayne thrust his arm under Blade's wrist, sending the knife flying across the room, disappearing under one of the water tanks.

Thayne smashed the heel of his other hand into Blade's nose, then stepped in, lifting the man off the ground, and dropping him into the nearest tank. Water sloshed over the side, but Thayne ignored it, moving on to Big Boy.

The large man had turned at the sounds of the fight. Big Boy tossed Emma aside and rushed Thayne with his arms stretched wide. Thayne prepared for the impact since there was no way he could avoid it.

He felt like he was hit by a cement truck as he was

crushed up against the cinderblock wall. Huge arms locked around his chest squeezing the air from his lungs. Thayne dangled in the air, similar to how Emma had, but Thayne was no way out of the fight. Fisting his hands together, Thayne raised them over the man's head and smashed them down on the back of his neck, repeating the action over and over again.

The world started to blur. Thayne slammed his hands down once more, and Big Boy sank to his knees. Thayne gasped in air as the bands around his chest loosened. He pushed the man back and brought his knee up smashing it into Big Boy's face. With the satisfying sound of bone crushing, Big Boy dropped to the ground.

Emma struggled to her feet but clung to the wall for balance. Thayne's instinct was to go to her. Instead, he looked to where Blade emerged from the fish tank. Thayne took a second to pull in another deep breath then attacked, not giving Blade time to get set.

Blade slashed out. Thayne dodged back, ready for the follow-up swing, which came at him immediately. Thayne blocked, knocking Blade's arm up and away, and thrust his hand under Blade's chin catching him in the throat. Unfortunately, it was only a glancing blow as Blade pulled back at the last instant.

More cautious now, the man came in on him. They moved around each other in an eerie kind of dance. Blade swung. Thayne leapt back. Blade slashed out again. Thayne dodged and came up against the lobster tank.

Thayne saw a slight twitch on the man's face and knew Blade thought he had him. Thayne waited, not moving until the man made his next strike. Thayne feigned to one side. As soon as Blade made a correction into it Thayne twisted back the other way, stepping in to land a solid blow to the man's chest, which seemed to stop Blade in mid-air.

Thayne on the other hand kept moving, catching the man with a jab to his face. Blade staggered back and then lunged. Thayne side-stepped it and whipped out his fist with another solid hit this time to the jaw, dropping Blade to the ground.

Thayne sucked in air as he waited a second to make sure the guy was down to stay before heading to Emma.

"Emma, come on. We've got to get out of here."

She looked at him slightly dazed. "But, those men—"

"Don't worry about them." He clasped her hand and pulled her to him, wrapping his arm around her, tucking her firmly to his side. She stared at the men on the floor. He could see her fright.

"We've got to go." He drew her away, heading for the front, not daring to go out back in case they had someone waiting. Once around the bend, he shifted their direction through the bar area. They cut through the next restaurant and out onto the sand.

Thayne kept her tight to his side, knowing it would look like a loving embrace instead of two people fleeing a fight. Emma's head was tucked against his shoulder. He laid his cheek on her head, curving his body around her. He could almost believe it was a loving embrace himself if it weren't for the trembling of her fingers in his, and the thundering of his adrenaline-jacked heart.

They'd almost got her. Anger seethed in him at his own carelessness. *All because he wanted one nice evening with her. He wasn't good for women. They weren't safe around him.* He berated himself every step they took.

"Thayne." Emma's voice trembled slightly, she was holding it together a lot better than he had a right to hope.

"It's okay, just stay with me."

"Where are we going?"

"I want to get farther away before we'll cut over to my hotel."

She stopped. "We should go back. We need to talk to the police. Those men need to be arrested."

"Don't worry about it." His mind was going over

everything he needed to do.

"Those men tried to kidnap me. They may try for other women."

Thayne felt the tremor rush over her. "No. Listen, don't worry about it. Just wait here for a minute, I have to make a phone call."

"You're calling the police?" She stayed locked on the idea.

"No." He pulled out his phone and hit dial. It was answered immediately.

"Thayne," Matt said.

"They went for her. Are we set?"

Emma spun and looked at him, her eyes wide. He caught her hand and tried to pay attention to what Matt was saying.

"Are you clear?" Matt asked.

"Yeah."

"Okay, it's all arranged. Tell me where you're at. I'll have the driver meet you."

"We're on the beach, headed for my hotel. Have him get her things and meet me there. We–" Thayne broke off as Emma pulled free.

"Who are you?" She backed away. In the moonlight, he couldn't tell if it was uncertainty or fear he saw in her eyes. One thing was certain – there was panic.

"Matt, I'll call you back." He reached out his hand to her as he disconnected the phone with his other hand. "Emma, it's all right. I just have to get us some place safe."

"Us." She picked up on the word. "You're involved in this?" She took another step. "You set me up. I am so stupid."

"No." He moved toward her.

Her hands came up as if to ward him off. "No!"

"Emma, I Promise I will tell you everything." Thayne ease forward. "Just not here."

"What are you involved in?" Her voice cracked.

"Not what you're thinking."

She shook her head. "Who are you? How did you...? Those men...? And why are you with me?" Her head tilted to the side as if she was trying to get a better image of him.

"They think you have something they want. Something that was meant for me, that you picked up by mistake."

"Something you have?" She was quick. Thayne thought with satisfaction.

"Yes, but they saw you get it so they are focused on you."

"When did you get it? Is that why you stayed with me? Are still with me?"

"No, I got it right after." He eased closer.

"So why are you here?" She shifted away.

"Because I was worried you'd be in danger."

"What is this? Some kind of spy game?"

"Some kind." He sighed. "Look we have to get out of here and somewhere safe." He edged in reaching out his hand. He could almost touch her again.

She glanced at his hand then shook her head. "No. Stay away from me. I want answers."

"I'll give you answers, just not here. We need to get you somewhere they can't find you." Too late he realized how that sounded.

"You ... no!" She spun and ran.

Again, Thayne was a second too late. He reached for her and missed. Emma sped away as fast as the narrow cut skirt allowed her. He hung back not willing to add to her panic. A sob carried on the breeze reached him.

Pain ripped across his heart. Thayne thumped his hand against his chest in effort to knock it away but it just drove the agony deeper.

He knew he deserved the pain and every bit of accusation in her eyes. He just didn't think the pain would be so bad. Thayne stopped dropping his head to his chest, laboring just to get in the next breath.

He wanted to call after her but couldn't. Nothing he could say would make it better, and he couldn't risk the men hearing and finding her. Thayne forced himself to follow her. He had to keep her in sight to make sure she was safe and he was close enough if she needed him.

Ahead, her feet dug into the soft sand. Her narrow bottomed skirt made it difficult for her to run or even keep her balance. She glanced back over her shoulder. With a cry, she went down, catching herself with her arms out.

Her head hung for a moment then came up and she peered at him. Thayne heard another sob and it ripped at him. He stopped. Her eyes met his, full of hurt and pleading.

Thayne started to take a step forward. She shook her head. He waited. She scrambled to her feet, dodging through the beach chairs now empty of sun goers. He let her get ahead before he followed, still not daring to let her out of sight, even with more people around the area. When she got close to her hotel, she cut across to it, taking the path that led around the pool area.

Lights along the path glistened off her hair. She crossed over a little bridge while he circled around the pool, disappearing into shadows. Emma didn't slow her pace. Hiking up her skirt, she took the stairs that curved up to her room two at a time.

He heard the door close before he followed her upstairs and listened at her door until he was sure there were no sounds of trouble coming from inside. Satisfied she was safe, he went below by the pool and settled into a lounger that gave him a clear view of her door.

Once more, he dialed Matt.

"What happened?" the man asked.

"Emma freaked. She ran. She doesn't trust me." The condemnation in his words was like a blow to him.

"What do you want?"

What did he want? That was a joke. He shoved his

hand back through his hair. *What he wanted was Emma safe and trusting in his arms.* "We have to move her."

There was a pause. "Agreed," Matt's answer reached him. "It could get hairy if you're caught kidnapping her, even if it's for her own good."

"Tell me something I don't know." Thayne said with a sigh.

"The place we set for you is on a private island out in the bay. The driver will pick you up and take you by boat out to the island. You'll stay there until you fly out. We're working on a new passport for her. Should have it late tomorrow or by the next morning."

"Okay. What's the driver's name?"

"James Brant."

"Well, at least you didn't say Bond." Thayne blew out a breath. "Have him go get my stuff and be waiting out behind her hotel in an hour."

"Do you think you can get her?"

"Yeah. I'll just have to practice my cat burglar routine."

"Just don't get caught."

"That's the plan."

"No, I mean really, don't get caught. I'm not sure what we could do to get you out." Matt's concern came loud and clear over the phone.

"I understand. I'm going to wait for it to settle down for the night out here and your guy to get into place before I make a go for her."

They talked over plans for a minute more, ironing out the details before Thayne signed off. He stared up at Emma's room. He'd made a mess of things. Worse, he'd hurt Emma. That was the one thing he hadn't wanted to do. He should have told her everything earlier that evening.

He was stupid and selfish. He'd wanted a few minutes for his own. Stupid. He wasn't good for women.

Pain ripped again at his chest. He closed his eyes. The

image of Emma tumbling onto the boat and into his arms filled his mind, followed by the one on Bond Island standing on the rock. Foliage framed her, the beautiful little bay behind, Emma, looking up at him in a sweet offering. He could almost hear the vows of love on both sides being said.

CR&

Emma fell back against the door as it closed behind her. She fought the sob that wanted to escape. How could she hurt this much? She'd only known him two days. She closed her eyes and Thayne's image filled her mind. How could she be such a fool to think that a man like him could be interested in her?

She was not going to cry.

Tears slipped free. She gasped a breath, trying to pull the tears back. She needed to think. Her mind went back to Thayne. Why did he have to feel so right? Wishful thinking. She shook her head. She needed to stop thinking of him.

Men were after her. They'd tried to kidnap her. Another sob rose within her and she swallowed it down. Emma looked at the phone. She needed to call the police. And tell them what – that two men tried to kidnap her because they thought she had something they wanted? But she didn't have it because the man who had saved her had already stolen it and she didn't even know what 'it' was.

She closed her eyes again trying to keep Thayne from her mind, not that it did any good, he still slipped in. His hand stretched out to her. Pain on his face, like it hurt him that she didn't trust him.

"No," she said aloud. It was a lie. He couldn't be hurt because of what she thought. He'd have to have feelings for her for that. He was deceiving her. She had to let it go. She had to be smart. She was supposed to be smart. Opening her eyes, she pushed away from the door.

The first thing she needed to do was make sure her

room was safe. She already should have done that. She moved around the room similar to how Thayne had done earlier when he walked her there after shopping.

Emma stopped in the middle of the room. The men at the market, on the motorcycle, it was an attack on her. No random snatch and grab.

Thayne had protected her, sheltered her with his body.

"Don't go there," she said aloud, but she remembered the jerk of pain when they'd hit him. He'd saved her tonight, too.

"Okay, so that meant he might be a good guy, but he was still using you." She tipped her head back as tears again slipped free to trickle down her cheeks.

She walked over and sank down on the edge of the couch. So what should she do? She didn't dare go anywhere. Her plane wasn't for another two days. Maybe she could catch a flight to Bangkok and stay with Paige. The idea gave her a rush of hope until she realized she couldn't risk bringing the danger to Paige. She lean back and covered her face. She'd have to stay.

The question was, was that safe? They'd already broken into her room. Her old room, she clarified in her mind, but it didn't bring her any relief. Or was that Thayne? No, she pushed the thought away. Something told her if Thayne had broken in, she would have never known he'd been there. She could definitely see the other guys doing it. The one with the knife came to her.

She shivered at the image of Thayne facing him as the blade slashed out. He could have been killed but it hadn't stopped him from taking on the man to save her. She groaned. She didn't know what to do.

A knock at the door had her jerking upright. Terror filled her as she looked at the door. The room remained quiet. She glanced at the sliding glass door. There was no escape, it just led to the balcony which was a good twelve foot drop to the ground or she could maybe make a dive into the swim pool.

There was another knock. "Emma."

She barely heard the voice. She stood debating on trying the balcony.

"Emma, it's Thayne."

She froze. She was safe. Emma took a step to the door then stopped again. How did she know she was safe? He could have alternative reasons for saving her. Maybe it was all a set up. He'd already deceived her.

Cautiously, she walked to the door and pressed her hand against it, fighting the desire to open it.

"Emma," he said her name again as if he knew she was there.

"Go away," she said so softly.

"Emma, we have to talk."

"No, go away." This time she said it louder so he could hear her.

"You need to listen."

"No, I said go away or I'll call the police." She caught her breath, knowing she really wouldn't, just not sure why. *So foolish.*

There was no sound from the other side of the door. She waited, still nothing. Pressing her eyes to the peep hole, no one stood there. He was gone. For some reason that made her feel more like crying.

What did she think he would do, break the door down to beg for her forgiveness? Emma buried her face in her hands and stood there a minute before pushing her self-pity away.

Taking a deep breath, she straightened, and thought about what he'd said earlier on the phone. It was about moving her. That she figured was a good idea. There was a huge amount of hotels on the island. She could move to a different hotel and neither Thayne nor anyone else would be able to find her before she went home.

Decision made, she went into the bedroom and lifted

the new suitcase she'd bought onto the bed. A twinge of pain hit her at remembering the time she'd spent with Thayne. It had been so fun, natural, right.

Emma shook it off and started gathering her clothes, laying them in the bag. It was easy because they were all clean and stacked neatly from being laundered, and the suitcase was much larger than the one she'd brought. She packed her souvenirs around the clothes then went to the closet to get the few items hanging there.

The bracelet on her wrist caught her attention. She went to work on the knot but no matter how she tried, she couldn't get it to come free. She thought of cutting it off but didn't have anything but her fingernail clippers. She reached to retrieve them when something caught her attention. Emma stopped and listened.

Nothing reached her but she could have sworn she heard a faint noise. She lowered the makeup bag she was holding into the suitcase and glanced back at the doorway. Again, she thought she heard a sound, but wondered if it wasn't that she was listening so hard for something that her mind conjured it up.

She looked for something to use as a weapon but had nothing. No mace, hairspray, not even a spiked high heeled shoe, so she picked up her brush and stepped cautiously to the doorway to the outer room.

Emma pressed against the doorframe and peeked around. The room was empty, then, as she watched an arm pushed the curtain aside.

Chapter Eight

Thayne stepped inside.

Emma threw the brush at him and made a dash for the door.

She heard a grunt then the sound of footsteps. She tried to ignore his approach and focus on the lock, but an arm snaked her around just as she reached the door. Her scream was cut off by a hand being clamped over her mouth. Emma stamped her foot down on his.

"Emma." Her name was ground out.

She drove her elbow back and heard a satisfying whoosh of air, but knew she was held too tight to do any real damage.

"Emma, stop fighting me. I don't want to hurt you." Thayne pressed her into the door with his body.

She struggled trying to break free.

"Don't fight me, love."

His final word snapped something in her. She twisted her mouth lose from his hold. "Don't call me love." She gulped in air. "Not when you don't mean it."

"Emma." Her name sounded drawn out with a touch of pain.

The hold on her eased, and he turned her to face him. Thayne raised his hand to cup her cheek. "Please, listen to me." His eyes were deep pools which seemed to hold such sorrow they pulled at her.

"No." She shook her head.

"Please." He brushed his thumb over her cheek bone. "Let me explain."

It was the sincere need in his eyes more than just his voice that won her over. She wasn't sure if she was ready to trust him completely, but he must have sensed enough in her that he tipped his forehead down to rest on hers and let out a sigh. After a minute, he raised his head and looked at her.

"I am sorry." He brushed his lips over hers.

When she tried to pull back, he let her.

"I didn't mean to hurt you." He swallowed. His hand slid down her arm to take her hand, and he tugged her toward the couch. "Come sit down so we can talk."

Emma let him draw her forward but couldn't help glancing back to the door.

"Don't think about it," he said.

She kept her gaze from him as they moved. When she sat, she wrapped her arms around herself to keep from reaching for him. She knew he would hold her if she did, and she knew she'd give into him, but she wasn't ready for that yet.

He didn't sit beside her but stepped several feet away and crossed his arms over his chest. He was quiet a minute before he started.

ᏣᏍᏬ

"I didn't mean to hurt you. That was the last thing I wanted." Thayne realized the moment the words came out of his mouth that was the wrong thing to say.

"What do you want?" The way she snapped at him was ruined by the tremor in her voice. "You already got what you came for. You already said that."

"I want to keep you safe."

She started to shake her head. "You don't have to worry about me. I can take care of myself."

"Emma." He reached for her hand, but she pulled it away. The weight inside him doubled. He pulled back his hand, and when she didn't say anymore, he finally asked, "What are you going to do?"

He didn't think she was going to tell him. He stood and crossed the room giving her space. Glancing through the open bedroom door, he saw her suitcase on her bed mostly packed. *Good, that would make it quicker.* "Where are you going?"

She glanced at him then away. "I'm changing hotels. You said I needed to move," she finally answered. Again her chin quivered ruining her bravado.

"That's a good idea. Have you picked one yet?"

She shook her head. "I thought that I'd just have the taxi drive around until I found one I liked the look of."

Thayne nodded. He continued his course around the room, stopping to pick up a water bottle off the table. "That's a good idea. Then they can't trace it from the phone call." He turned his back, twisted off the cap, and slipped a small pill he pulled from his pocket inside the bottle. He waited a second for it to dissolve before turning and walking back to her.

Emma took the offered drink automatically and downed some.

"There's only one problem with that. How do you know the taxi you'll be getting into isn't the people after you?"

He saw her gasp as the possibility hit her. Her hand trembled as she raised the water bottle and took another drink.

"I ... I don't." She looked at him. He could see she wanted to turn to him, ask him for help. He could also see the pain holding back her trust.

"Emma." He sat on the couch beside her. She didn't pull back. "Let me help you."

A tear slipped out at the corner of her eye. It was his undoing. He wrapped his arms around her, easing her against his chest.

"No." She resisted a second than crumpled in his arms.

Thayne buried his fingers in her hair and rocked her. "It's all right, sweetheart," he whispered the words, pressing a kiss to her temple.

"Don't call me that when you don't mean it."

"I do, love."

She leaned back a little in his arms and studied his face. "Thayne?"

"It's all right. I will do everything I can to keep you safe. Give all I have. Please trust me."

She shook her head.

His heart plummeted until he realized she wasn't shaking no, but trying to clear her mind. Her hand locked on his arm to steady herself though he had her snug against him. There was no way he'd let her fall.

"Thayne?"

"Are you all right?"

"I feel so … tired."

"Just let it go. I promise to watch over you." He eased her back to him. She sighed and rubbed her cheek on his shoulder.

"That's it, love."

"Don't say that. Don't mean—" She went lax.

"I do."

Thayne couldn't resist holding her for a minute. She felt so right, perfect in his arms. With a sigh of his own, he eased her back on the couch. He stood looking down at her, then leaned over and pressed his lips to her forehead. She didn't stir.

It only took him a few minutes to pack the rest of her belongs, and check over the room. Satisfied he had everything he closed the bag, put it by the door, and checked the time. His ride should be waiting. He dialed the number Matt had given him.

"This is James. This is Mr. Bond I presume," the man said in way of greeting.

Thayne shook his head. "You have got to be kidding me."

"Matt said you'd like it."

Thayne rolled his eyes. "Are you in place?"

"Yes, and I have your stuff."

"Great. Can you come give me a hand?" He gave him the room number and disconnected.

A minute later, there was a knock at the door. He opened it to a young Thai. "James Brand at your service," the man said in excellent English with just a touch of a British accent.

"Can you grab her bag and purse?" Thayne motioned to them before stepping back to the couch to lift Emma into his arms.

The man looked concerned. "I was told I was taking you to a safe house."

"You are. I just don't want a scene to attract any unwanted attention, and she's not real happy with me right now."

Thayne could tell the man was thinking it over. Finally, he nodded.

Thayne felt a wave of relief. "Can you make sure the way is clear as we go?" He hoisted Emma higher on his chest, curved her into him, so her head was on his shoulder, and followed James out. At the corner of the building, Thayne waited until James motioned him on.

Thayne was tense as they approached the alley, but fortunately the way was clear. James opened the door of the newer-model car before going to put the suitcase into the trunk. Thayne lowered Emma in then slid in beside her, resting her back into him. James closed the door, got in, and they were off.

There was still quite a bit of traffic but not so much that Thayne had a hard time watching for a tail. Fifteen minutes later, they pulled up on a peer and drove almost to the end. James cut the motor and came around to let him out. Thayne once more carried Emma.

Getting on the boat was a bit tricky, but the calm water helped. Thayne laid her on the bench and turned to take the suitcases. In under two minutes, the motor was going, and they were headed out over the water. Thayne sat by Emma, easing her into his lap. She didn't move at all. Luckily, it was a relatively smooth ride.

"This is it," James spoke up swinging around a small private island. With the bright, full moon Thayne was able to get a pretty good look. He figured it wasn't much more than a quarter mile across. Three sides had rock and cliffs that led to the water, but as they came around the other, it revealed a small beach and a pier. He could make out three houses built halfway up the hill.

"You're in the one on the right," James said as he pulled up and docked at the pier. "It's fully stocked. I checked it out already."

The hike up the hill carrying her was difficult, but there was no way he was going to have James carry her for even a little while. He was concerned that she stayed unconscious. He didn't think she had drunk that much, but Emma didn't stir at all, even when he laid her down on the large master bed and eased a pillow under her head.

As much as he wanted to remain with her, he went back out to speak with James.

"I need to get back to town," the Thai man said. "If you need anything call. I will be out later tomorrow."

"Thanks." Thayne watched him go then proceeded to go through the house locking the layout firmly in his mind. There were three bedrooms, each with their own master bath. Two opened out onto the deck with the pool. The kitchen, dining and family rooms were one large, open area that looked over the water.

There was a deck built on stilts that ran the entire length of that end of the house, giving a spectacular view. The nice thing was with the deck and the thick jungle growth going up the hillside behind, it would make the house very hard to sneak up on.

Satisfied, he went back to check on Emma. She was in the exact same position as he'd left her. He sat down and checked her pulse. It was good.

Once again he was surprised she was unconscious. Either she was extremely reactive to drugs or she was so exhausted her body just decided to give out. Probably both, he decided. He couldn't believe she'd made it through the whole boat ride without waking, though it was probably a good thing. He had a feeling she wasn't going to be happy with him when she woke and found he had kidnapped her, even if what he was doing was for her own good.

The sad thing was; he felt like he'd been making progress in getting back in her good graces − before he'd drugged her. Unfortunately, he hadn't been sure she would have agreed to go with him and he'd felt he was running out of time. Three attacks in one day said whoever else wanted the information they thought she had were getting desperate.

Thinking of the chip made the spot where it was attached to his hip itch. He forced himself not to scratch it. Thayne looked down and picked up a lock of her silky hair, letting it slid over his finger. He wanted to caress her cheek but held back the motion, reminding himself she wasn't his to touch, no matter how much he wished it was so.

He slipped off her shoes then stood, looking down at her. She was so beautiful, but it was something more that got to him, and he wasn't even sure what. He just knew he didn't want to lose her. Thayne sighed. That meant he had to win her.

He crossed the room and opened the doors that led out onto the balcony. A breeze came off the water cooling the air and carrying the smell of the plumeria trees by the pool. He left the doors open and walked slowly across the tile to the balustrade that kept the jungle back.

The sound of water was faint, but the view amazing. He wished Emma was awake so he could show her. The moon glistened across the water, and there were a few lights in the distance. He closed his eyes and let the calm feeling wash over him.

He was tired. The evening before, he'd been too worried about Emma to get much sleep. It felt like he'd been going non-stop for far too long. He rested his elbows on the rail and let his head drop to them.

The image of Emma slipped right back into his mind, not that it was very far. Funny, a week ago he hadn't even known her. A week ago he'd told Matt he didn't want a woman in his life, and he'd meant it. He also meant what he'd said about not being good for any woman.

Thayne rubbed his hands over his face. He still wasn't good for women to be around, specifically Emma. She was in danger because of him. Thayne straightened, looking out over the water.

After a minute, he let out a sigh, went to one of the chaise lounges, and settled down to watch. He was not going to let any harm get to Emma. That included from himself. As much as he wanted and dreamed, she couldn't be his. And, he did dream of her, and a family, and a happy, long life of love.

C3&C

Emma woke slowly to a chorus of birds. She stretched, feeling utterly content and very relaxed. She could smell the sweet gentle fragrance of plumeria she'd come to love. She wondered if she could get them to grow back home. It should be possible. They had other plants growing here that did.

She stretched again and sighed. Cracking open her eyes to let in the early morning light that filtered into the room through the fine, filmy, curtains that billowed out in the gentle morning breeze, which kept the room from being stifling hot. She sighed again taking in the elegant surroundings. She was studying the painting on the wall when it dawned on her it was unfamiliar, as was the whole room.

Men trying to kidnap her, the thought rushed into her mind with images of Thayne fighting them off. It all flooded back with the realization that she should be in her own room and this was not it. It was not even the new room the hotel had moved her into.

Thayne. He'd brought her here, wherever here was. Anger, more than fear, spiked in her. He'd brought her here without her knowing it, but how? It hit her immediately. He'd drugged her. Panic started to climb but his promise rang out in her mind.

'I will do everything I can to keep you safe.' He would. She didn't doubt that, but he'd kidnapped her.

She pushed up from the bed feeling totally alert, without any lingering dizziness. She found herself dressed in the same clothes from the night before, except for her shoes. Looking over the edge of the bed, she found them waiting there. Bypassing them, she slipped from the bed. She waited a second in case of a wave of dizziness hit her. It didn't.

Emma walked to the door, her feet making no noise on the smooth tile. She peeked out. The house was still and empty. She turned back to where the curtain billowed in the breeze. Walking to it, she caught the light material and slid it to the side.

"Oh," the sound escaped her as she took in the view. It was amazing. Blue sky and water stretched out in front of her, dotted with several foliage covered islands, and an array of bright-colored boats.

Only a few steps away, a pool with cobalt tiles glistened in the sun. The area was framed with an array of trees, some flowering, other taller trees had orchid plants fastened to them with flowers cascading down.

To one side, there was a pagoda with two chaise

lounges under it. There were several other lounges and chairs around the pool and a couple tables. It was stunningly beautiful, but when her gaze landed on the man asleep on one of the loungers, he kept her whole focus.

Emma wanted to be mad and rant, but couldn't as his promise came back to her. He would give anything to keep her safe. She didn't doubt that, even if it meant his life. She caught her breath. Thayne would die to protect her.

She might not be able to be mad at him, but she didn't have to like the underhanded way he'd gotten her here. Now she wasn't so panicked, she could see his reasoning clearly. She had lost it, but in her defense, it wasn't so much fear but hurt that he'd lied to her.

'I do mean it.' His other words slipped through her mind. For a minute, she wondered if they were real. Had he really called her 'love' and meant it, or was it just wishful thinking, or a dream?

She tried to think back, but it was so fuzzy in her mind. She could remember the tender brush of his lips across her forehead, and the feeling of love that came off him. That was real, her heart yelled.

Emma crossed the area slowly, studying the man. Her heart pulled at her. He looked more peaceful than she'd ever seen him. His sandy-colored hair was in disarray, whether from sleep or running his fingers through it, she didn't know.

He, too, was wearing the same clothes as the evening before. His tan legs extended out from shorts that came to his knees. The hair on his legs showed golden in the morning sun. Thayne still wore his shoes, low-topped, lightweight hikers, good for water, walking and climbing.

Several buttons had come undone on his shirt letting her see hints of the sculptured muscles of his chest. She longed to trace her finger over the hard planes, instead she shifted her gaze to his face.

Stubble darkened his jaw. Again, she longed to trace

and caress his strong features. He had great eyelashes for a man, a nice nose, and amazing lips. She remembered the feel of them on hers and her heart jumped.

Her heart had been locked away so long ago, she figured she would never know love, but love had found a way in on its own. The realization hit her hard. She loved Thayne.

Emma pulled the certainty around her and settled on the edge of the chair, cautious in her movements, afraid of startling him. After seeing him fight, she didn't doubt he could do damage if reacting on impulse, where consciously he would never hurt her.

Thinking that, she figured she'd be wiser calling his attention and waking him from a distance, but she also wanted to glimpse the first moment of true feelings in his eyes when he awakened. It might be stupid, but she thought it might work. She could see before he had time to mask them.

Carefully, she laid a finger on his cheek, stroking it down over the stubble on his jaw. He didn't jerk but his eyes opened to reveal smoldering heat. A smile crested his lips.

"Emma," he whispered her name and raised a hand to bury it in her hair at the base of her neck. He applied slight pressure as he leaned up to meet her lips. They feathered over hers.

"My Emma." He breathed out like giving thanks, and she knew he meant the words in his heart, as he closed his lips over hers.

Emma slipped her arms around his neck as his free arm went around her waist to draw her in. The kiss continued long and deep. She felt herself sinking into him when abruptly she was pushed back. She found herself sitting on the lounge alone as Thayne scrambled up on the other side and moved several feet away.

"Emma, I'm sorry. I shouldn't have done that."

She wanted to object, but before she could, he turned and stalked around the edge of the pool, putting it as a barrier between them.

"I didn't bring you here to seduce you."

Emma was about to point out that she was the one that touched him first, but he didn't give her time.

"I know you must be mad and frightened." He kept his gaze from her and paced the length of the pool. "I promise, you're safe. You have nothing to fear from me. I won't touch you again. I'm sorry. I shouldn't have done that."

"You already said that. And I'm not scared. I already figured out why you did it. You said you were going to take me somewhere safe. Though, I wish you hadn't have drugged me." She gave him a minute to deny it but he looked uncomfortable, so she stood and went around the pool after him. He moved away before she could reach him.

"I'll see about fixing you something to eat. Just give me a minute." He walked into the house.

Emma wanted to laugh at him running away. She wasn't sure what just happened, but she had got the answer. There was no faking what was in his eyes when he'd first looked at her, or the way he'd said her name when it slipped from him. Thayne did care for her.

She didn't know why he'd broken off the kiss and then refused to look at her, but she had a good idea. Thayne was a man of honor. As he saw it, she was under his protection, was his responsibility, so he would guard her even from himself. She was afraid it might be something more though.

Emma walked to the rail and looked out over the water. Her thoughts remained on Thayne. Something ate at him, she knew that, could feel it, a pain deep within him. She'd sensed it before. She wanted to ease it, to wipe it away, but how?

Emma stood for several minutes before she heard him come out. She wasn't any closer to an answer. Turning, she found him waiting by the table where a tray rested. As she walked toward the table, she saw the tray only held one glass, one plate with sliced pineapple and melon, a bowl with what looked like muesli, and a small carafe of milk.

"You're not going to eat?" She watched him.

"I will later."

She wasn't surprised by his words. "Then you might as well take that back in. I'll wait and eat later with you."

He glanced toward her. "There's no need."

"I'm in no hurry. I can wait until you're ready to join me."

That drew his attention. He shifted his gaze beyond her to the water.

She let him have a minute. "Thayne," Emma said softly.

He didn't let her say more. "I'll get another bowl." He turned abruptly and went back in.

It was a bit longer wait until he returned. Emma didn't move to sit down until he placed another tray identical to hers on the table, then went and settled in a chair. He sat next to her.

Thayne was tense, but not how he was when he was on alert. This tension was a deeper, internal wariness. She didn't pry, figuring she had won one battle and needed to give him time before she started on the next. She might have steered clear from love in the past, but now, she'd met a man that she was willing to fight for. She had no doubt that Thayne's love was what she'd been waiting for and dreaming of all her life.

"You know, I think the little pineapples they have here have ruined me for pineapple for the rest of my life. They are so good." Emma tried to start a conversation.

When he didn't say anything, she continued. "And the little bananas. Do you have any idea where to get them in San Diego? I've never had them before."

"I don't do much shopping," he finally said.

"Not much of a cook?"

There was another pause like he was trying to hold back but words slipped free from him. "I don't mind cooking. I like grilling, but I haven't spent much time around home to do it regularly."

Emma felt a wave of hope. "So you travel a lot?"

"I have been for the last few years." The answer came easier.

"You said something about retiring or changing jobs. Was that true?"

"Yes. It's time. I'm ready for a change."

"So this is your last job?"

She had to wait again before he nodded. Thayne pushed abruptly back and stood before she could ask anything else. "I think I'm going to swim now."

Emma watched him walk away feeling a sense of loss.

She pushed her food around her plate a moment before giving up and carrying the food back inside to put away. The small kitchen had more of an American flare than European. It was well laid out, with a small work island in the middle and bar counter on the side, separating it from the dining area. A step down divided off the seating area. Emma didn't pay it much attention, her focus behind the closed door next to the room where she'd awakened.

Several more minutes passed before Thayne stepped out of the room. He didn't look her way as he crossed out to the pool. He dropped the towel he had over his shoulder onto one of the lounges up under the pagoda before diving smoothly into the water.

Emma couldn't take her eyes off him as he glided through the water. Though his strokes were precise and graceful, there seemed to be an inner tumult about him. It pained her, especially because she felt she was the reason for it.

As Thayne executed a flip turn in the water, heading back the other direction, Emma set off on her own. She went to the bedroom to where she'd seen her bag, and pulled out the swimming suit she'd bought with Thayne's encouragement, and went into the bathroom to change.

She paused, looking in the mirror. She liked what she saw. Though the swimsuit was technically a one piece, it was a bit more daring than anything she normally wore. It was fitting because what she was about to do was a great deal more daring.

With a deep calming breath, she walked out the doors onto the deck. Thayne still did laps. If he realized she was there, he made no indication. She laid her towel on the chaise next to his and settled down to wait.

Ten more laps and Thayne showed no sign of stopping. Her nerves spiked. Five more and she felt her courage falter. Did he really care for her or was it just her own foolish love leading her into wishful thinking? Emma thought about the feel of his lips on hers and wiped the doubt away. As he completed another turn, she stood.

The water was warm when she stepped down into it, but a welcome relief from the humid air, even though it was still early morning. She dipped down to her chin then, in an inverted breaststroke, swam out to place herself directly in his path as he closed to the wall one more time.

Water flowed around his body as he cut through it. She watched his head tilt up to catch a breath before dipping back into the water. His arm came up around for another stroke, driving him close.

Emma readied herself for the body blow if he didn't see her in time to pull up. Thayne's hand stretched out in front of him. The instant his fingers made contact with her, he pulled up. Shooting from the water in an effort to stop, his wake carried him into her. Emma was ready for all but the feel of him as he came up along the length of her.

She gasped, then gasped again as his arms wrapped around her.

"Emma." Her name burst from him, and he sucked in deep breaths his swimming had robbed from him.

He started to pull back. Emma wrapped her arms around him and hung on. His gaze went to her face. Before he could pull away or say anything more, she kissed him like she'd never kissed any man before. She put her heart and soul into the kiss and Thayne reacted in kind, accepting her offering and returning himself.

Chapter Nine

Thayne groaned as his arms tightened around her, molding her along the length of him. When his hands came up to frame her face, joy like Emma had never known burst in her, then abruptly, she was pushed away again.

"No." He tried to move back but she pushed off the side and grabbed his arm.

"Thayne."

He looked at her, his inner pain blatant on his face. Instead of letting it drive her away she pulled herself to him.

"Thayne," she repeated his name gently this time.

"You need to stay away from me." He ground the words out.

"No. I don't think that's what you want."

"What I want doesn't matter," he snapped.

"Yes, it does," she said just as forcefully, all her hesitation shattering.

"You don't know what you're doing."

"Yes, I do. I'm standing up for something I want. I love you."

Pain flared to agony in his features. "Don't."

"Why?"

"Because you don't mean that. You can't."

"I can and I do."

He was shaking his head, but that didn't explain the quivering she felt in his body.

"Thayne," she said gently, bringing her hand out of the water to touch his chin.

His attempt to pull back was ruined as his lips brushed her fingers in a kiss. He jerked, breaking free, but he didn't get far as she caught him with easy strokes.

"Tell me, I want the words," Emma demanded as she caught hold of him again. She knew if he denied her it not only would break her heart, it would destroy her. She would never let another man in the place reserved for him.

"It's better that you stay away from me."

She'd lost. Despair wave over her. "Why?" The word burned her throat.

He shook his head and looked away.

"Please tell me." Everything broke apart in her. "Make me understand because for once in my life I'm taking a chance. I have hidden myself away, never let myself get close to anyone. I've been so afraid of getting hurt that I've never let myself feel, but somehow you have snuck under all my defenses. Whether you like it, or even I like it, I'm in love with you. So, if you're going to deny us, I want to know why." Unfortunately, the water they were standing in did nothing to mask the tears that flowed down her face.

He cupped her cheek, brushing the tears away with the pad of his thumb. He shook his head but didn't say anything, just looked at her, his eyes caressing her as if to take her in so he would never forget her.

Pain again washed over her. "Last night you called me your love. Was it a lie or did you mean it?"

"You were so out of it. You weren't supposed to remember that."

"Why? If you didn't mean it."

"You don't understand. If I care for you, you'll die."

"What?"

He looked away and back and shook his head.

"Thayne," she whispered his name not sure how to break through the torment she saw there.

"I can't let anything happen to you." The words seemed to be pulled from him. His head dipped to rest on hers.

"Nothing's going to happen to me," she said gently, stoking her hands up and down his back.

"You don't understand." He looked up, meeting her eye to eye. "I was married. Her name was Beth, and she died because of me. In an accident meant for me."

Emma wasn't sure what to say. His pain was so palpable. She could not only feel it, but could taste it, and it left her sick. She reached up and cupped his face just as he did hers. "Tell me." She didn't want to say the words but they came out.

He took a deep breath, closed his eyes then opened them. "Beth and I married about seven years ago. She was an attorney. She handled a patent that I applied for. By the time the patent was finalized and sold into production, we were married. She knew I was an engineer, but what she didn't know was that I also was working for the government. You could call me a trouble shooter, though I didn't really do much shooting." He tried to make it sound like a joke but it came out hollow.

"I was pretty good at being discreet. We'd been married about two years when I went on an assignment overseas, and Beth decided to come surprise me." He pursed his lips before he continued. "We'd been struggling a little. Funny thing was I had already decided to quit the agency, so I could be around more. I wanted to start a family but with her career, she wasn't sure she was ready, especially with me gone so much."

Emma felt her insides lurch at what she knew was coming.

Thayne took a deep breath and continued. "Beth arrived, and I tried to get her to go home. She got mad and stormed out, grabbing the keys to my car on her way, said she was going shopping until I could be civilized and talk about it, which meant seeing things her way. The car was run off the road. She died. A witness said it looked like it was forced off the road on purpose. They'd mistaken her for me."

"I'm sorry." Was the only thing she could say, and she meant it.

"She died because of me. I thought I was keeping her safe. Keeping her from worrying." His voice broke.

"No. It was tragic, but you weren't responsible."

"If I'd told her."

"Nothing would've changed."

"She wouldn't have come running after me trying to save our marriage, afraid that I was having an affair because of my secrecy."

Emma figured he hadn't meant to say that. "She didn't know you well if she believed that. You would never have cheated on her. It's not in you."

His eyes softened as he looked at her, and his thumb again caressed over her cheek. "I won't let anything happen to you," he repeated the promise he'd already made.

"I know that. The only thing that worries me is you not giving us a chance – me a chance."

"Emma."

"Just tell me, last night when you said you cared, did you mean it? Do you care for me?" Emma put it out there. When he didn't answer, her heart began to ache. Maybe she had gotten it wrong. It wasn't the first time.

"Yes." The word was torn from him.

Her heart soared, and she went for it all. "Do you love me?"

"More than I can believe." His head dropped, and he covered her mouth with his.

His kisses were feverish, like a dying man and she was his salvation. Emma was only too happy to give him back life. She just prayed her life would be enough.

Emma had no idea how long it was before his lips left

hers and traveled down her chin to her neck, and the soft skin there. His hand ran over her back molding her to him. He buried his face into her and locked her against him, holding her like he never wanted to release her.

She wrapped her arms tight around him. Holding him close, stroking his neck and shoulders, willing all the sorrow he'd kept inside away. Praying he could feel her love and that just maybe, it would be enough to ease him, that maybe there was a way she could find a way to slide into his damaged heart and heal him.

There was a shudder from deep inside Thayne, then a groan followed by her name which sounded like it was ripped from the depths of his soul. "My Emma." It came again, this time in reverence.

His lips again touched her neck, lingering. Soft kisses stole her breath and made her heart pound. Her head tipped back offering him better access. He kissed his way down to her collar bone and traced the curve of it before following her throat up over her chin to her lips once more. His kisses were slower, deeper as life flowed in each one. He groaned out, raising his head.

Emma opened her eyes to look up and meet his gaze which seemed to caress over her. "Love," he whispered the word, a declaration, pledge and promise.

"I love you," she said back, meeting the next kiss as it came. She was so lost in him that when they slipped and dipped under the water, she really didn't care until the need for air penetrated her.

Thayne brought her out of the water and struggled to get his feet under them. "We're going to drowned ourselves." He gave a half-laugh. The eyes that looked down at her no longer held pain. "Come on, we better get out of this pool." He gave her one more, swift kiss before propelling her toward the end of the pool and the steps.

He caught her hand leading her out. She was slightly surprised when he led her to the pagoda and the chaise lounges.

"We need to talk." Thayne looked very serious. He picked up his towel and laid it out. When she went to follow suit with hers, he took it from her and dropped it on the other lounge, then caught her hand again and sat, pulling her down with him.

"This may not be a smart idea," he said settling her alongside him. "You are way too sexy in that suit." Thayne caught his breath as he looked at her. "What was I thinking? I'm going to kill myself." He kissed her then pulled back. "No more of that. We need to talk and plan. Maybe you better go sit on your own." He didn't release her, just turned to face her, putting space between them, but holding her hand in his.

He stared at her for a full minute, not saying anything.

"Thayne?"

"I'm an engineer. I like things thought out, and you are playing havoc with my thinking. Here it is. Number one: I have got to keep you safe. I cannot let anything happen to you. It would kill me." He brought her hand up to kiss her knuckles. "Number two:" he paused to take a deep breath. "I do love you, and as soon as this is over, I'm going to retire. That was already planned, but I'm going to marry you."

Emma felt laughter rise within her.

"What?" he looked at her.

Happiness welled up. "I think you're supposed to ask me first."

He smiled. "I will, but I need to get a ring first." He touched her cheek with one finger. "Will you say yes?"

She nodded.

"You've only known me a couple days." He pointed out like it would make any difference.

"You've only known me a couple days."

"I've known from the minute I saw you. That's why I couldn't let you fall anywhere but into my arms."

"Oh." Emma couldn't say anything else.

His lips twitched. "Besides, I have a full file on you. I know everything there is about you, Emma Anne."

Emma wrinkled up her nose, and he laughed. It sounded good coming from him. "That's not fair."

He kissed the end of her nose. "I'll get you a file on me when we get home."

"Edited?"

"Just a touch. There are a few classified things."

"Is it that easy to retire?"

"Actually, I retired from the government about a year after Beth died and went to work with a friend who set up a private consulting firm." He accentuated the title. "We do work for the government and company espionage. It paid extremely well."

"And was dangerous enough," she added knowingly.

He shrugged his shoulders and drew in a breath. "For a long time, I didn't care."

"Now?"

"I'm ready to try life again." He shook his head. "It's funny, I was quitting because I didn't think I had the heart for it anymore, but what was happening was destiny having something else in mind for my heart."

"Destiny?"

"I think I was meant to meet you. It's the only explanation."

"That's not very scientific, Mister Engineer."

"No, but it feels right."

"Yes, it does."

He kissed her again. "I've got to quit doing that. I can't think of anything but making love to you when I do. And, that's not going to happen until this is all over and we're married."

Her surprise must have showed because he continued. "You have waited this long. We'll wait for couple days for it to be right."

"I–"

"No. You're worth the wait, love." He kissed her again then pushed her back. "You better go over to your own chair. I don't know if I can handle a heavy make-out session and survive. It's been a long time for me."

Emma wasn't sure what he was saying, but he answered for her.

"I haven't been with anyone since Beth."

Pleasure came with the knowledge. Emma kissed him then slipped from his side though she really wanted to remain next to him. Thayne reached over and caught her hand once she'd settled back on the other chair.

"So what do we do now?" she asked.

"Wait. Our flight leaves tomorrow night."

She shook her head. "But my flight's in the morning."

"It's been changed so we're on the same flight. Also I'm getting you a new ID."

"What? How?"

"Pulling some government strings. Don't worry. You won't get into trouble. It will be totally official. I'm afraid we'll have to hang out here, though. I don't want to run the risk of going into town. I'm sorry to have to ruin your vacation."

She shrugged. "Spend the day on a beautiful, exotic island or a packed city. I'll take the island."

He smiled. "You have all your shopping done?"

"And then some, thanks to you yesterday."

"Okay. What do you say to taking a walk?"

"So you can check things out?"

"Yes. I like to know the lay-of-the-land. Then we can come back, eat, swim and just relax."

"Sounds perfect."

০৪৪৩

Thayne watched Emma pick up a shell from the little beach. She looked back over her shoulder at him. Love surged up. She loved him. There was no doubt. It was in her eyes. The only way she hadn't given herself to him was physically, and it wouldn't be long until then. He just wanted to be free from his past before that happened.

Destiny. Emma was right. He'd never believed in it before, but he knew he was meant to meet her. It all played out in his mind, from seeing her and having her fall into his arms, to her being the one who picked up the magnet.

She rose and stepped back to him. "What are you thinking?"

He reached out and caught the lock of hair that had come free from her braid and hung alongside her face. "Of destiny."

Her lips tipped up gently just before she turned her head to kiss his hand. "I'm think, I believe in destiny now, too. It's either that or I'm afraid it's all a dream, and if it is, I don't ever want to wake up."

"It's real. More real than I've felt for years." He eased in to kiss her. He couldn't seem to get enough of her. She wore a filmy cover over her swimsuit now, but it didn't hide much from him when his mind had her locked firmly in it. "Have I told you this morning, how beautiful you are?"

That seemed to take her by surprise. He remembered she thought of herself as a − what was it, something like a kind of pretty smart girl? He made a mental note to tell her everyday how beautiful she was. That shouldn't be hard because she was.

"Let's see if I can prove to you how real things are." In a quick movement, he reached and snagged her around the waist. She let out a little yelp which was cut off with his mouth. After a moment, he raised his head and sighed, resting his forehead on hers. "You are so kissable." He sighed again in the pleasure of just holding her.

She snuggled into him. "I've never been kissed this much in my life. I like it."

He felt like laughing. "Good, because I plan to do it a

lot."

"I like that idea." She pressed her lips to his then laid her head on his chest, her arms wrapped around his waist. "What will happen when we get home?"

He thought for a minute. It seemed simple to him. "First, I'll hand off this chip and sign my resignation papers. We'll find you a ring. That's if you want to help pick it out, since you're the one that will be wearing it the rest of your life. Then, we better drive up to meet your parents. It's only right I ask them for your hand. When do you have to be back to work?"

"Not until next Monday. School's out right now and I'm only at the hospital part time. Two to three days a week."

"Nice. That will give us plenty of time together. Do you mind the idea of a quick wedding? Am I rushing you?"

She shook her head, but he caught her chin stilling it. "No. I want you to really think. I want it to be what you want."

"I want you."

Her words slid over him bringing a wave of pleasure and need. "Oh, love." He kissed her then stepped back, holding his hands out to ward her away. "Let's go for that hike."

She laughed when he turned and walked away from her.

Thayne didn't care. He needed space. She was far too delectable. "So how much time do you need to plan a wedding?" he asked over his shoulder and prayed it wouldn't be months. His first wedding had been planned for ten months. He didn't think he could handle that with Emma and stay honorable.

"I don't need a big ceremony."

"I thought women wanted that." He glanced back in time to see her shrug.

"I get kind of shy in front of crowds. I know, funny for

someone who does speech. I mean I can do it, and I even give lectures, but for our wedding, I would kind of like a private quiet setting, then maybe a reception later on."

Thayne pictured it immediately, standing in a gazebo, water and greenery around them, sayings their vows that would make them one forever.

He stopped and turned, catching her hand in his. "A quiet ceremony it is." His voice felt rough as he said the words. He wanted to kiss her again. It seemed he couldn't keep from doing that. Instead, he turned and led her along the path.

The first trails they followed were wide, probably traveled heavily by the people that stayed on the island. They led around the houses and to the beach. One led up above the rock cliffs giving them an amazing view. They could see Phuket and the big Buddha that set on the hill over it. Cut off by the jungle, they couldn't go any farther, and it was getting hot so they turned back

On the way to the house, they discovered another smaller trail but since neither had eaten much breakfast they decided to eat lunch first before seeing where it led. After, they also changed into walking shoes and Thayne picked up a machete that was in the stand beside the door.

Emma arched a brow at him.

"I figure it's here for a reason."

"Unless this place comes equipped for psychopaths."

He grinned at the comment.

"It's getting hot," she said as they stepped out.

"That's an understatement. Without the light breeze off the water it would be unbearable. They're heading into the monsoon season. I think we're in for big rain this afternoon. We better hurry."

One thing he found out about Emma that he really liked was she liked to hike and wasn't afraid to get dirty and sweaty to see things.

They walked around the house and took the path that

lead up the hill. It was steep going. At first the path was wide making it easy to walk on. They'd gone about half way up when it forked. They decided to take the right path first. After going another thirty feet, the trail cut across the island and came out on the cliffs just up from where they had been earlier, giving them another view of Phuket.

"That is still so beautiful here," she commented.

"It is. Did you get to go up to the Big Buddha?"

"Yes, Paige and I did on our second day here. We hired a car to take us all around. Did you go there?"

"Yes. The day before I met you. Did you see the monkeys there?"

She laughed. "Yes, there was one sitting in a garbage basket, drinking from a soda can."

"When I was there one got a lady's purse."

"I heard they did that. That's why my bag crosses over my shoulder. Not as stylish but harder to lose or get swiped."

"Smart." He caught her hand and pulled her too him, snaking his arm around her. With things cleared between them, he had this insatiable need to hold and touch her that was eating at him. He hungered to make her his. Luckily, it sounded like she wasn't going to make him wait forever, he thought with relief. He would wait as long as she wanted, but he might go insane.

She tilted her face up to him, and he took it as an offering, capturing her lips. Her fingers lifted to the nape of his neck to run feather-light strokes that he felt to his heart. A small groan escaped her, feeding his need.

His control threatened to slip. He broke the kiss. There was a dazed look in her eyes and a softness the shouted of love that she didn't try to hide.

Thayne pressed one more kiss to her cheek before he stepped back. "We better go."

He caught her hand leading her back down the path to the other fork. He had to release her as they started up this one. It was narrower, obviously less traveled. It climbed almost straight up. Several times they had to grab the ground for hand holds.

"Be careful gripping plants," he cautioned. "I don't know if any might be poisonous."

"I understand. Also, let me know if you see any spiders."

"Like that three-inch guy over there." He pointed high in a tree to the side.

"Exactly. I'd already seen him and several others. I can say spiders are not my favorite things, or the six-inch long centipedes."

"I think they're millipedes."

"Either way, they have way too many legs and are way too big. I don't even like the small ones we have back home."

"Don't like bugs?"

"Actually as long as they don't get on me or in the house, I don't mind them. Fair warning, so you know any spider higher up than my shoulder is your responsibility after we're married."

He laughed.

"Hey, I'm totally serious. I had a deal with my brother growing up. I took care of anything that might start growing in the fridge if he took care of the spiders."

"Fair warned. I promise to slay all spiders for my lady."

"Thank you."

"It will be my pleasure. Anything else?"

She thought for a moment. "No, not really, I can handle most other things I can think of."

"Snakes? Mice?"

"I can't say I want to handle poisonous snakes but the others don't bother me, or mice. I can even handle if a bird gets in the house."

"A bird?" He laughed.

"It happened to one of my neighbors? She'd left the sliding glass door open. She was freaked out, came out of the house screaming."

"So what did you do?" He just knew she handled it.

"Put on a pair of leather gloves, went in and caught it. It had trapped itself by the window, so panicked it wore itself out. I just picked it up, took it outside, and released it."

"I'm impressed."

"Thank you."

They continued. The trail became rougher, almost choking out in spots where the foliage attempted to take back the land. Thayne had to use the machete to cut a way through. Sweat poured from him. They stopped often to drink from their water bottles before continuing on.

They crested the top of the hill and started down the other side. The sound of water lapping up on the shore grew louder, but it was hard to gage their location because of the thick foliage. Suddenly, they broke out on a rocky out cropping only about six feet from the water. There was a sandy patch not big enough to be called a beach.

"You want to wait here while I go check it out?"

"I can make it." She started down not waiting for him.

"What a woman," he let out.

She looked up at him and grinned. "You haven't seen anything yet."

"But I'm liking what I'm seeing." He followed her down.

The rocks were wet from high tide and the going was slow. They reached the postage stamp sized bar of sand, and he moved to survey it, then kicked off his shoes and waded out ten feet. The water went up to his knees. It would easily be doable to bring a boat in. He didn't like the fact that someone could sneak onto the island from behind, but he figured someone would have to be very familiar with the island to know about this spot.

He turned to find Emma watching him.

"Is it okay?" she asked as if understanding what he was thinking.

"Yes. I just wanted to check it out." He walked back toward her. When he stepped up on the beach she went to him, sliding her arms around him.

"Are we in danger?"

"I just like to be cautious."

She nodded accepting his answer then glanced at the sky. "In that case, we better hurry."

He looked at the dark clouds boiling over the mainland. A gray wave of rain descended out of them. The downpour was heading their way.

"You're right. Let's go." He went up the rocks first then lowered his hand to pull her up the last part. They hiked faster than they had coming, pushing through the growth, though watching all around for spider webs and danger.

At the top, the rain was already over the water and nearing rapidly. They stopped only a minute to gulp down the rest of their water and catch a quick breath before heading down the other side.

When they reached where the forks came together they put on more speed, almost running down the trail. Overhead, the sky turned black. The foliage thinned and they saw the house. They were only about fifty feet away when the sky opened up and water spilled down. It felt like someone was throwing buckets of water on them.

Thayne urged Emma on in head of him. Emma reached the cover over the entry and turned to him, laughing. Delight sparked in her eyes. She wiped hair back from her face.

Life radiated off her, and he couldn't stop himself from wanting to catch it. He laughed as he wrapped an arm around her and pulled her to him. He couldn't remember ever feeling this light and carefree.

"Nymph." He crushed her lips with his.

Her arms encircled him, and he pulled her off the ground. She gasped but didn't break from his lips. He took advantage by delving into her mouth, deepening the kiss. Each time he kissed her, it seemed to grow more intoxicating. He wanted more, needed more. He hungered for her like he never had another woman. The way love poured off her, he didn't doubt she was his, just as he was hers.

When he lifted his head, he still couldn't bring himself to release her. Her face glowed with pure joy.

"A lifetime won't be long enough." He let the words he was thinking slip out.

"Then it will have to be forever." She lowered her head back to his.

Chapter Ten

When Thayne lifted his lips from Emma's again he let her slide down his body to touch the ground. He couldn't bring himself to release her, so he kept her hand in his, leading her around the deck to the chair under the covering. Hand in hand, they sat and watched the rain.

Thayne disappeared inside to bring out a couple pastries he'd seen in the fridge earlier and new water bottles. The rain continued for about two hours before the sun came out making everything glisten with a fresh, washed glow. They found a deck of cards and realized they both like games. After several games, they stretched out on the chaise lounges under the pagoda to take a nap.

Before dinner, they took another swim, which was punctuated with rounds of kisses that left them both hot despite the refreshing water. The food left for them was a mixture of chicken, vegetables and rice, which they savored while sitting on the patio, learning more about each other.

Now open, conservation flowed easily between them as they cleaned up together. Putting the last glasses in the cupboard, Emma was caught from behind by strong arms.

Her gasp turned into a moan as Thayne's lips skimmed her neck. "Mmm…"

"Exactly," he said against her skin. "Have I told you what a beautiful neck you have?"

"No." Her answer squeaked out along with shivers of delight at his words and the tantalizing feel of another kiss.

Emma never knew her neck was so sensitive, but when he brushed the spot right under her ear, her knees went weak and another moan escaped her.

"Enough of that." He pushed her away, but kept his hands on her hips to steady her.

"You're the one who started it." Emma fought to get herself back in hand. Wanting to step back into him almost swamped her.

"I know, I'm killing myself. No more touching your neck until we're married." His eyes burned. "Maybe I should say no more touching you."

Emma turned to him. For a moment, Emma was afraid he was serious, but before she could think of an objection, he stepped in and gave her a quick hard kiss. When he pulled back he held her hand. "Let's take another walk."

They took a stroll down to the beach then up to the point to watch the sunset.

Emma took pictures to catch the beauty of the island then some of him until he swiped the camera to take pictures of her with the glow of the setting sun on her. He even managed to get some good photos of them together thanks to the timer on her camera.

It was getting dark by the time they made it back down the hill, but they were able to follow the trail easily enough. Once more they settled on the deck to talk until Thayne caught Emma yawning.

"Why don't you head to bed?" he suggested.

"What about you?"

"I think I'll stay out here a while longer," he said gently. Standing, he extended his hand down to her.

"Are you going to sleep out here again tonight?" Worry flashed in her eyes.

"No. I wasn't really planning on it last night. I just fell asleep."

She paused, the tension that had spiked in her body shifted. "While you were thinking?"

"Yes."

She stepped closer to him. "About me?"

"Yes." Even in the dark, he could see the glint in her eyes.

"You had decided it wasn't safe for me to be around you."

Thayne almost pulled back. She read him like no one ever had before.

Her hand came up to rest on his chest. "Maybe I shouldn't let you be out here alone."

He smiled. "Don't worry. I'm afraid you won't be able to get rid of me now even if you wanted. You've not only convinced me I can't live without you, you have me addicted to your kisses." Thayne added a teasing tone to the words but he could still see the worry in her eyes. He wrapped his arms around her. "Don't worry, love. No more fighting myself. I want forever with you."

She visibly relaxed and leaned up to brush her mouth over his. "Sorry. I'm not used to being in love. I'm afraid I'm going to wake in the morning and find I dreamed it all."

"You mean guys trying to run over you with motorcycles and kidnap you?" His lips twitched.

"No, that you might actually love me."

"Believe me. That is real. Though, I will be the first to admit, I never would have believed it of me. I didn't want it to happen," he clarified. He kissed her, and then walked her to the door, opening it for her to go in.

She looked back to him, her eyes filled with longing that was open for him to read. He was tempted to give into it. He knew if he pressed, she would come to him, but he also knew it wasn't right.

Emma needed to carry his name before he could make her his. It was as important to him as it was to her. He brushed a final kiss across her lips then brushed them with the pad of his thumb. "Sleep well, my love."

A smile glowed on her face as she turned from him. Thayne watched her through the filmy curtains for a moment before forcing himself to move away. He walked around the pool to the railing much the way he had the night before, but tonight, he was at peace within himself.

He looked out over the water and sighed. Contentment washed over him. Maybe he could have love in his life.

He forced himself to straighten though his thoughts lingered on Emma. He made a final sweep of the area around the house before heading inside. He needed sleep. His concern for Emma had kept him from getting much rest the last few days. Thayne stretched out on the bed and let the dreams of the future with Emma at his side fill his mind.

ᘓᕷᘔ

Thayne's eyes snapped open. His senses alert. He didn't know what awakened him, but he didn't question his instincts either. Something was amiss.

He slipped silently from his bed and pulled on the pants and shirt he'd left ready out of habit, for such a need. He stepped into his shoes and snagged up his backpack. In under thirty seconds, he was heading for Emma's room.

She was sleeping on her side, her hands clasped under her chin. Her hair was still in the braid she'd worn earlier. She looked so peaceful, but he didn't let it make him hesitate. He leaned over her then dropped his hand over her mouth.

"Emma," he whispered in her ear as he felt her jerk awake, her mouth trying to part to scream. She stilled instantly. "Good girl." His thought slipped out as he sought to reassure her. "Pull on some clothes and shoes as fast as you can."

He barely waited for her nod before he turned, and crossed to the open French doors. He studied the deck before he slipped out the door. Scanning the area, he silently made his way to the railing.

The moon gave enough light to pick out images from below. He wasn't surprised to see another boat bobbing by the dock that hadn't been there earlier. The shadows of at least two men stood on the dock.

As Thayne watched one tied off the boat and one more man climbed out. He was about to head back to the house when he became aware of Emma coming up behind him. By her small intake of air, he knew she had caught sight of the men below.

He turned reaching for her hand. "Come on. We have to go."

She followed him without question. He led her around the house to the path. As he moved, he pulled his cell-phone out of his pocket, brought up the number and dialed.

"James, we have a problem." He didn't wait for the man's comment. "Men are on the island, heading for the house. We're taking a path over the hill. There is a small rocky beach on the other side, almost directly across from the house. We need a pickup."

"I'll get there as soon as I can," the man said and Thayne cut the connection.

Thayne came around the corner of the house just as a figure stepped off the path from the beach. Thayne was the first to recover from the surprise. He shoved Emma back and stepped forward to slam his fist into the man's face. It was a good hit. The man dropped to the ground.

Unfortunately, the altercation gave time for the other man coming up behind him to prepare. Thayne barely got his arm up to block the strike that sent him stumbling back. Thayne recovered, blocked the next fist thrown at him and sent his own plowing into the man's midsection. The man staggered but didn't go down. The man dropped his shoulder and rushed at him, driving Thayne back against the house.

Thayne jerked up his elbow catching the man across his cheek, opening a cut. Thayne followed the motion by jamming his knee up. The man dropped to the ground. Thayne turned in time to see the first man had made it to his feet and was going for Emma. Thayne dove for him.

The man spun swiping out his hand. Thayne caught the glint of metal in the moonlight and tried to twist away. Whether he was too slow or the man read his action, Thayne felt pain spike in his side. He didn't let it alter his actions. He continued around swinging out.

The man pulled back at the last second, so Thayne only landed a glancing blow, but it gave him the moment he needed to set himself. As the man moved in again, Thayne was already in motion. The knife blade whipped past him, cleaving nothing but air. He pivoted bring his leg up slamming it into the man, lifting him off the ground and dropping him back several feet.

Thayne didn't slow to check for damage. "Emma," he called her name and caught her hand as she reached for him. They ran, taking the path headed up.

For the first fifty feet the foliage was light, having been tamed back, but as they started to climb, the growth thickened around them. Thayne knew from their afternoon walk it was going to get worse. They moved as fast as they could, trying to follow the path. He wished he dared turn on a light but didn't, afraid it might give away their location.

He didn't delude himself on how long of a head start they might have. They had one advantage. They'd climbed the trail earlier and knew where they were going.

He was impressed how silently Emma moved with him. She didn't hesitate or comment. He pressed for more speed. She matched her pace to his and climbed, putting her trust fully in him.

Pain rippled through his side. Blood had soaked his shirt and now ran down his side. Thayne brought his free hand up, pressing it over the wound. Biting his lip was all he could do to keep any sound from escaping. Behind him, Emma faltered a step as if alarmed by something, but she didn't speak. Still, the motion of his arm stretched back to her, pulled on his side.

His foot caught a root, unseen in the darkness. He stumbled slightly, jerking his arm. This time, a hiss slipped through his lips before he could swallow it down.

"Thayne?" Emma whispered his name barely louder than a puff of air.

"Keep going," he whispered back.

She did. After a few more feet, he had to release her hand because of the tiny tugs on his side from each step. He missed the hold on her instantly, but knew it was for the best. They had to get over the hill. He had to get her to safety.

Pressing down harder on the wound, he tried to staunch the blood flow. Fire burned in his side. He didn't think the cut was very deep but it was probably two to three inches long. His main worry would be infection from tramping through jungle, even if it was a relatively a short distance. He'd worry about that later, after he got Emma to safety.

They reached the fork in the path. "Go." He hissed the word to her and pushed her onto the path heading up. He started on the other, when she grabbed his hand. He knew she registered the blood on his fingers by her reaction.

"I'll be right there," he whispered. "I want to leave a trail." He placed his foot in the junction of the paths, and pressed down and turned.

She hesitated, watching him, then placing her feet very carefully. She walked up the trail until she disappeared from his sight. Good girl, the thought ran through his mind.

He took several more steps, again pressing hard into the soil before coming back, walking as cautiously as Emma had. In the daylight, he knew it probably wouldn't fool anyone, but at night, following by flashlight, he hoped it would buy them at least a few minutes.

Emma was waiting about ten feet up the trail. He

edged past her to take the lead again.

"Thayne?"

He caught the question and worry in his whispered name. Still she fell in behind him without making a fuss. They hadn't gone far when they heard the noise of people on the trail. They froze, both holding their breath until the noise shifted. It was evident their pursuers had taken the other path.

The higher they climbed, the rougher it got. Emma's hand rested on his back, not to push him forward, or for him to help pull her up, just touching him, as if she needed the contact with him. He could understand that, and he took reassurance in that touch.

Twice he lost the path and had to use the penlight from his backpack to find it, filtering the light through his fingers to go on.

"We need to check your side." Emma whispered the second time they stopped.

"Not yet. They're still too close."

"You're still bleeding. That's not good."

"Not yet," he said again, started off not giving her time to object further.

She fell silent. He knew she didn't like it, but caution and common sense held her. He also knew the cut needed to be tended. It wasn't a serious injury, or it would have laid him out by now, but she was right. The bleeding hadn't stopped, and he was starting to feel the toll it was taking on his body. It was only his need to protect her that kept him going.

CR∞

Emma wanted to sag in relief when they crested the hill. It had been a lot different climb than their earlier hike. Her nerves were still on edge from the attack at the house. At first, it was all she could do to keep panic from rolling over her. Having Thayne there and the need to be strong for him kept her in check.

Adrenaline had helped, too, then she found out he was injured and everything in her focused on that. She wanted to know how bad it was. He seemed to be moving all right. His breathing was good but she could sense his pain. Every once-in-awhile, Emma picked up a slight intake of breath, or a stiffening in him.

They made it about thirty feet down the other side when she couldn't take the fear anymore and caught his arm, stopping him.

He tensed and whipped back. She didn't let his action get to her. "They can't see us. We need to look at your wound." The hill blocked the moonlight, and the foliage made it almost completely dark, but still Emma could tell he wanted to argue, then he relaxed slightly.

"We have to be fast." He turned on the flashlight, again shielding it with his hand. When he angled it to his body, it showed the lower section of his shirt and top of his shorts were soaked with blood.

Fear shot through her. Emma caught her breath, steadying herself. She reached out and eased the material away, revealing the cut that was about the length of her finger. It had split the skin, but luckily didn't seem to be too deep. Still it should be stitched up and had to hurt.

Thayne slipped off his backpack, unzipped a pocket, and pulled out a first aid kit. Emma took it from him, opening it. The stuff in it wasn't just the basic stuff, she realized after a quick inspection. She removed a couple antiseptic pads and cleaned the area.

Thayne hissed out a breath as she worked, then handed her a small packet of ointment that he'd split the seal on. When she was done with that, he held out a clear filmy bandage type thing. Spending time in the hospital, she saw them all the time, usually over IV's. They were waterproof bandages.

She placed it carefully so it covered the cut completely and was smooth to the skin. There was more she would've liked to do, but at least, it was tended and sealed from anything getting in it.

Thayne pulled out another small packet and swallowed the pill from it. "Antibiotic," he said as if to reassure her.

"What about something for the pain?"

He shook his head. "I have to remain alert."

"Ibuprofen." She lifted the bottle from the pack and dumped a couple in her hand.

Wordlessly, he took and swallowed them. She handed him a water bottle then put the first aid kit back while he downed two-thirds of the contents. She finished the bottle off when he handed it to her. He slid the backpack onto his shoulders.

"I can–" she started to say but was cut off with a shake of his head. Exasperating man, the thought barely made it through before his head dipped and he pressed his lips over hers. He was there then gone, already turning to head down the trail leaving her heart pounding.

Emma followed. It wasn't hard to keep up. Their pace was actually slower than it had been previously. The trail was rougher and the foliage so thick there was no way to see to make it through. Emma stayed right with him, her hand touching his back as much for comfort as for a guide. She tried not to think of the three-inch spiders hanging in the trees and six-inch millipedes on the ground. It was enough to think about the men behind them.

She wondered how many there were. There'd been two at the house, but there had been another two down by the boat. Were all four after them? Had one remained behind? Had Thayne injured the two bad enough they couldn't come after them? That thought gave her a second of hope before reality slipped back in.

They wanted her. Wanted what they thought she had. What would they do to Thayne if they caught them? Was he considered expendable? Just muscle hired to protect? He was definitely dangerous. He'd proven that.

Would they figure he might have it? Did he have it? She didn't know. She didn't even know what the 'it' was, or at least what was on it.

Frustrated, Emma wanted to scream 'leave us alone'. She wanted to enjoy her vacation and the love she'd found with Thayne.

The growth around them started to thin. They were getting close to where they'd have to climb down the rocks.

Emma thought she heard a twig snap. Thayne stopped in front of her so fast she found herself plastered against his back. He reached an arm back to her, but remained silent, listening, then pulled her forward, quickening their pace.

Emma almost fell over an exposed root. It wasn't the first time, but she stubbed her toe hard enough she had to bite back the exclamation that almost slipped out.

A touch more moonlight filtered in, giving the area a faint glow as they reached where the hillside dropped off to the beach. Emma knew it would be trickier climbing than it had been earlier when she could see the hand holds. Luckily, it wasn't too far to the little beach. As if reading her thoughts, Thayne turned to her, leaning close.

"I'll go first." The urgency in his whisper added to her tension. "Follow right behind me. I'll be there to catch you."

She wanted to ask, 'what if you fall,' but didn't have time, as he turned back and placed one foot over the edge. There was a rustling of leaves behind her. Emma spun. A form burst from the foliage toward her. Emma couldn't keep back the scream at the odd, misshapen face barely visible in the shadows.

Arms reached for her. She tried to pull back but wasn't fast enough. A hand locked onto her arm, jerking her to the man. She swung out her free hand only to have it knocked away. The kick she went for next was more successful in connecting but didn't seem to do any damage. She was so close to the face now, that she realized the man wore some kind of a headset.

Abruptly, she was pushed to the side. Emma landed hard by the edge of the drop off. Behind her she heard a grunt and rolled. At first, there was one big dark shape moving around, emitting grunts and groans, but as she watched, she could pick out the two different forms.

Thayne was taller by a couple inches, but the other man looked bulkier. Emma wanted to cheer when she saw Thayne hit the man followed by a kick. There seemed to be no affect.

When the man hit Thayne in the side, close to where he'd been cut, Emma cried out. Thayne staggered, but recovered. He hit the man, knocking away the goggles. Before her hopes could rise, Emma saw another form rush forward.

She cried out in warning and launched herself at the man, who spun on her. Wrapping his arms around her in a bear-hug that forced all the air from her body, he lifted her off the ground and shook her.

Emma was aware of another man passing them. Behind her there were more sounds of struggles. She knew Thayne was now facing two attackers. He'd face two before, but now he was injured.

Emma slammed her forehead into the face of the man holding her like she'd seen on TV. She was rewarded with a burst of pain in her head, but also a satisfying grunt. Released so fast, she had no chance of catching herself, she dropped to the ground a second time, gulping in air.

She lifted her head in time to see one man strike out, but she couldn't tell who. The man he hit staggered back, but one of the other men took his place. This one she could tell was wearing the odd goggles. The man plowed into Thayne knocking him back like a lineman. For a second, Thayne teetered on the edge of the drop off then he went over.

"No," Emma screamed, springing from the ground to

make it to the edge. Before she could go over, a hand locked on her shirt hauling her back. She clung to a rock as the material dug into her neck. She couldn't take her eyes off the still form barely visible on the sandy patch below. She cried out as she was ripped free from the ground and hauled up to stand.

"Where is it?" A low rumbling voice demanded.

Fury flared in her. "Where you'll never find it." She shot back with more bravado than she knew she possessed.

"Really."

Emma heard the sneer in the voice as it answered back.

"I'll think you'll tell us. Let's go," he said to the other men.

"What about the body?" One of the other men asked in a nasally voice and odd accent.

"Leave him," the man holding her snapped.

Emma shuddered at the term 'body'. *No, Thayne couldn't be dead.* The image of his still form wavered in front of her eyes. Water lapped near his fingers on one hand. Darker shadows of rocks were near his head.

Emma squirmed against the man holding her. She needed to go to Thayne. The only thing it gained her was another rough shake.

"She wouldn't have trusted it with the stooge. He sure got more than he paid for, the shmuck. Even if the tide doesn't pull him out to sea, it'll be days till anyone finds him, and they'll just think he fell climbing where he shouldn't have been."

Emma could see one of the men replace the goggles on his head. He swore. "I can't see anything. He broke them." He pulled the head gear back off.

Emma finally figured out what they were – night vision goggles. They allowed them to move through the dark easier.

"You'll just have to stay close," the man who seemed to be in charge said.

"She smacked her head against mine and cracked the edge, but they're still working." the man holding her said.

Emma became aware of the trickle of blood that ran down the side of her face. The throb of pain in her head got lost in the agony of leaving Thayne as the men propelled her up the path. Emma baulked, digging in her heels. There was a smack against the back of her head that sent her stumbling forward, only to be shoved onward again when she stopped.

Tears stung her eyes, blurring her vision, not that she could see anyway. She was helpless and being taken away from Thayne. She wanted to go to him. She refused to believe he was dead. No, he would be all right. He would find her. Emma clung to that hope as she was forced on, shoved every time she was too slow in taking another step.

Emma figured they were over halfway to the top when she thought she heard the faint sound of a boat. Her hope surged. It had to be who they were meeting. They would find Thayne and get him help. She wanted to turn and run but, trapped between the men on the small path. There was nowhere to go.

Chapter Eleven

Thayne's head pounded, ripping him into consciousness. He became aware of the damp, hard-packed sand under him and the salty smell of the ocean. His effort to shift to a more comfortable position brought a spike of pain in his side and the memories of what happened. "Emma," he choked out her name. There was no answer.

He rolled to the side and pushed himself up enough to look around, ignoring the throbbing in his head. He was on the little patch of beach but there was no sign of Emma. She was gone. They'd taken her.

Dizziness and nausea hit him, forcing him to lower his head to his arms. It took him several breaths to get control of the pain that threatened to wipe him from consciousness. He couldn't pass out. He had to get to Emma.

Moving slowly and using the cliff for support, he struggled to his feet. The world spun around him for a minute, but with deep breaths, it steadied. He raised his head to study the climb. It seemed insurmountable but Emma was there, and he had to get her before they got her off the island, and he lost her forever.

Terror hit him. How long had he been out? Looking at his watch, he figured it wasn't long. Thayne put a hand on a rock to pull himself up when the sound of a motor reached him. He turned to the water, straining to listen. After waiting for a minute, he was certain it was headed toward where he was on the island. Hope poured through him.

James.

He'd lost the flashlight he'd been carrying, so pulled another from his pack and shone it on the water then cut it off. He did it a second time before James caught the idea and cut his lights, moving in closer.

"Hurry, I'll guide you in." Thayne waded out. He turned on the flashlight to illuminate the rocks. "They've taken Emma," he said as he gripped the side of the boat. James cut the engine and reached to help pull him up.

"You all right?" the Thai man asked.

Thayne wanted to yell no, they had Emma, and he wouldn't be all right until he had her back safe in his arms. "Yeah," he said instead. "Just have a master of all headaches. We've got to get to the other side of the island before they do."

To Thayne's relief, James didn't argue or even ask questions. He just backed the boat away from the shore and headed into deep water. James kept the speed low to cut down on sound. It also gave him a chance to see obstacles in the water, since they were running dark, with only the moonlight to guide them.

Thayne used the back of the passenger seat for support to move around until he could drop into the seat. He pulled off his backpack and dug into the first-aid kit again, dumping a couple more ibuprofen into his hand. He swallowed them, once more discarding the need for something stronger.

When they reached where a rocky point jutted out, Thayne had James back off the motor and let the boat drift.

"There were four that landed but only three that ambushed us, so they must've left one with the boat. With the climb they have to make with Emma, we should have at least an hour before the others make it back. There's a spot over there where I can make it onto the shore, and the trail that leads to the beach and dock. I should be able to take the guy by surprise easy enough."

"Do you want me to go?" James volunteered.

"No." Thayne didn't want to endanger the man's life any more than necessary. Besides, he wasn't willing to risk Emma's life with anyone else. "Wait here until I signal you, then bring the boat up. We can hide it behind the big cruiser and wait for the other guys to get there with Emma. I'll need your help then, but we'll have surprise on our side."

James let the boat drift a little closer into shore, but kept it well away from the rocks. Thayne dropped his backpack in the bottom of the boat and slipped over the side, entering the water silently and ignoring the pull of pain on his side.

It took him less than a minute to swim to where it was shallow enough to wade to shore. By the feel of rocks and coral under his feet, he was glad he'd left his shoes on. He waited a minute, crouched low in the water but detected no sign that he'd been seen. Deciding he was clear, he made the short run to the foliage and followed the edge of it until he reached the trail. Thayne figured the whole process took him about eight minutes.

The moonlight showed brighter on this side of the island, which was a blessing and a curse. It made it easier to see where he was going, but also meant he could be seen. Still, the thick growth gave him plenty of cover.

Thayne hurried along the path, slowing when he neared the beach. The dock was at the far end. Fortunately, there was another section of trail that looped around the foliage closer to it. Thayne paused at the beach opening to survey the layout. It wasn't hard to spy the guy. He was stretched out on the nose of the boat, leaning back against the windshield. His arms were folded behind his head and it looked like he was asleep.

This time, Thayne slipped along the trail with more caution, moving like a ghost in the night. Before breaking into the open, he paused again. Now he could actually hear soft snoring coming from the man.

Thayne remained bent over as he sprinted across the sand. He placed one foot on the dock and pressed down. No sound came from the structure. Still, he moved with care, placing each foot carefully.

Thayne was four feet from the boat when he stepped down on a board that creaked. The man on the boat moved, lowering one arm. He started to sit up, but it was too late.

Thayne sprang across the distance separating them. The man hardly got a squeak out before Thayne grabbed his leg and pulled him off the boat. The man hit the dock. Thayne slammed his fist into his chin, and the man went limp.

Thayne jumped on the boat. It only took him a second to find a rope to tie the man up and gag him with an old rag. He took some satisfaction knowing the cloth would taste awful.

Finished, Thayne shoved him off the far side of the dock, down on the sandy beach, so those coming down the trail wouldn't see him. The man lit on the sand with a dull thud. Thayne jumped down beside him and pulled him in close to the dock, obscuring him, then climbed onboard and found a flashlight, flicking it a couple times.

A minute later, James eased his boat up to the dock. "Nice," the man said as he climbed out. "What's the plan now?"

"We wait. They're using night-vision goggles, so we probably won't get any lights for a warning. I don't think they had infrared, though. How about you take our guard's place napping on the front of the boat? You're about his size. I'll wait by the rock cropping there." He pointed to a shadowed spot about eight feet away. "Another good thing is, I don't think these guys have guns, but they do like knives, so be careful."

James stepped on the boat and pulled out an emergency paddle. He held it up and smiled back.

"Not a bad idea." Thayne grinned. "How about getting me one of those?"

James tossed the one he held and retrieved another for himself then stretched out on the front of the boat, similar to how the man had been.

Thayne took his position by the rocks. Fatigue threatened to swamp him but his thoughts went right to Emma. She had to be all right. Fear of what they'd do to her settled like a hot brick in his stomach. He'd been in enough bad spots and seen enough to know how bad it could be.

Thayne couldn't stand any of those things happening to her. He had to get her back. He needed her. He loved her. There was no denying it. He would spend the rest of his life letting her know how he felt. Another fear trickled in. Maybe after all this, she wouldn't want him anymore.

The image of Emma looking up at him, gentle, loving, filled his mind and eased his heart. She would still love him.

❧

Emma's heart pounded but not from exertion. The vision of Thayne on the sand played over and over in her mind. He'd been so still. It wasn't that far of a fall, she tried to reassure herself. All she could do was pray he wasn't dead; and that the boat she heard was the man who was to pick them up. She prayed he'd come ashore and found Thayne.

How bad had the knife wound been? Thayne said it wasn't bad. But, it had still been bleeding before the fight. She shivered. He was hurt and needed her.

Tears burned her eyes. Under the thick canopy of trees, she couldn't see anything but the blurred shape of the man in front of her. The island seemed to have fallen silent except for the heavy breathing of the man behind her. He puffed in her ear with every step. Shivers ran down her back. Emma closed the gap with the man in front just to escape the creepy feeling, not that it would give her any true comfort.

She had to think of some way to escape. She didn't doubt, if they got her off the island, she was dead. She'd be fish food or worse. She definitely didn't want to think of the worse.

Her foot caught on something, jerking her from all thoughts as she fell forward. She was going down. Rough hands grabbed her arm, keeping her from hitting the ground fully, then he jerked her up so hard, Emma thought he'd dislocated her shoulder.

"Keep moving." The words grated over her. He shoved her forward, almost making her trip again.

"I can't see." She struggled to get the words out. "I need to rest."

In way of answer, she was pushed again. The action caused her to stumble. She caught herself then thought why not go down. She wanted to delay them as much possible. Though she didn't know what difference it would make, Emma dropped to the ground.

"Up."

Emma didn't see the kick coming. It hit her in the side sending spears of pain through her body. She cried out and curled into a ball. It wasn't an extremely hard kick, but it knocked the air from her.

"Don't bruise her, yet," The man in front snapped.

The 'yet' brought more fear than the kick had.

"Get her moving then."

The large man, who was in front, reached down and lifted her off the ground. He set her on her feet and wrapped one meaty hand around her wrist tighter than any shackle. He started forward dragging her up the path.

Fortunately, the pain in her side settled into a dull throb. Still, panic rose within her. If he had a hold of her, there would be no way she could escape. Every step wrenched her arm and already sore shoulder. At least, the man who'd been breathing down her neck fell behind enough she had some respite from him.

She stumbled over another root, and her arm stretched out enough she cried out again. The man slowed his pace. Emma tamped down her fear and tried to think of a way to escape. The only chance was to get away and hide in the growth. But, with her wrist trapped, there wasn't much chance of that. Then there was the problem of three against one. She had no fighting skills, and due to the goggles, they could see and she couldn't.

She wanted Thayne. The thought of him tore across her heart. *Please, let him be all right.* The cry echoed in her mind. She was still locked so firmly on it she didn't register the man holding her wrist stopped until he jerked her to a halt.

It took Emma a second to realize they'd reached the top of the hill. The trees opened up enough she could finally see. To one side were the lights of Phuket. In front, the moonlight glowed over the water. Emma made out the dock far below and the three boats that were tied there.

She couldn't let them get her to the boats. As if hearing her plea, the hand holding her wrist dropped away. Emma pulled her arm to her chest and locked her other arm over it in case he reached for her again. She rubbed her wrist.

"Come on. We need to get off this island. We've been here too long." One of the men grumbled.

Emma saw the big man look back at her and tightened her arms to her body. He gave a light shrug dismissing her and moved off down the path. Aware that the man behind her had just reached the top, Emma hurried down the hill to keep distance between them.

The moon lit this side of the island letting her move easier. As she continued on submissively, the men seemed to become more lax. The space between her and the man behind her opened farther. Nearing the fork in the trail, she eased her pace just a little, spreading out from the man in front. Though she'd been watching for it, she didn't see the fork until the big man passed it.

She took in a deep breath, filling her lungs. Emma tensed as she neared the fork. One more step. Like a runner when they heard the sound of the starting gun, she bolted onto the side path. She ignored the leaves and branches that whipped out of the darkness like ghostly hands. Behind, she heard the shouts as the men reacted in pursuit.

"Let me pass," one of them demanded. "I'll catch her."

Emma fought for more speed. She heard a ruckus on the path behind her. It gave her a second of hope. Two more strides, adrenaline pumped in her. She hit her toe on a rock hard enough to bring tears to her eyes. She breathed through the pain, barely catching herself as she stumbled.

Footfalls pounded the ground heading her direction. There was nowhere off the path she could hide, especially since he could see in the dark. She tried to picture the trail from earlier. She had to reach the cliff, then she could take the other trail back to the house.

It was either that or hope the water was deep enough that if she could jump far enough out to get beyond the rocks, she might survive the plunge. She wondered if she really could survive the fall because she was willing to risk it, if necessary.

A large leaf hit her in the face. A cry escaped her. The crashing through the heavy growth sounded closer. In front of her, the way cleared. She could make out the cliff edge.

A grunt behind her was the only warning Emma got before she was hit. Arms locked around her, pitching her forward. The force knocked her off her feet, smashing her to the ground.

Air whooshed from her lungs. Lights flashed through her mind. Emma wanted to let herself slip into them only to be yanked back by a hand locking into her hair. The man pressed her face into the moist earth.

Emma picked up the stench of decaying vegetation just

before she was flipped over onto her back. She didn't see the hand coming at her until just before it connected with her jaw. Lights flashed before her eyes. This time, she slipped into them, falling into darkness.

CROSS

Emma swung in waves of dizziness and nausea. A jarring motion expelled every breath she managed to catch. She tried to shift to fight the odd feeling, but found herself trapped. It took a moment to realize her head was hanging down, that the iron bar across the back of her legs was a muscled arm, and the repeated blows to her stomach were impacts with the large, sweaty shoulder she was draped over.

With the world around her clearing, the throb in her chin picked up. Emma got a hand up to touch it. It was sore, but when she moved her jaw, she decided it wasn't broken. She felt awful, but worse was not getting free.

She struggled, hoping the man would let her down. Instead, she received a shake that jammed her into his shoulder. She gagged. Emma wished she'd thrown up. It would have served him right but unfortunately, all that came out was a groan of pain.

She closed her eyes to think. A tear slipped from the corner of her eye. They were still on the island. How much time had passed? Opening her eyes, she tried to look around.

It was still very dark. Besides the path and foliage, she couldn't make out anything, then she heard the gentle sound of water lapping on the shore. They had to be close to the beach. She shuddered. She had to do something, but she couldn't even left her head.

Moonlight flooded in around them, lightening the shadows. The man's footsteps slowed, more sluggish but no less jarring. The plant growth ended.

The beach! Emma screamed the word in her mind and started to struggle again, not caring what reaction it gained her. She wasn't going to let them take her without a fight.

"Wake up."

Emma heard one of the men say, then the sound of a creak from the wooden dock. She squirmed harder, banging her fists on the man's back. He ignored her as if she was nothing but a pesky nuisance, as he strode over the sand. Emma gouged her fingers into flesh but there was little give in the muscle.

Her head dropped in defeat. That was when a commotion exploded around them. Ahead of her, from the dock came the sound of something hitting flesh and a loud splash.

At the same time, a shadow erupted from the sand onto the man directly behind her. Hanging upside down was an odd angle to figure out what was happening. Something extended out from the shadow. The short man who had kicked her shifted, but was too late to escape the attack. Emma heard a loud whack. The man staggered back and dropped.

The shadow turned her way, moonlight cut over it, bringing the image of Thayne to life.

The man holding her charged forward, starting to throw her aside. Emma shifted on her own, but instead of trying to get down like a moment earlier, she locked her fingers into her captor's hair and held on. He bellowed as she pulled. Behind her she saw Thayne smash his fist into the man he'd previously hit as the man tried to rise. The man dropped back onto the sand.

Emma lost track of them as the man she was holding swung in Thayne's direction while twisting, trying to dump her off. She hung on as he gripped her legs and forced her up, throwing her backward over his shoulder.

He grunted as she ripped hair from his head as she fell. She landed on the ground behind him, flat on her back. Emma rolled aside as the man rushed at Thayne.

Thayne swung what looked like an oar. The man raised

his arm, blocking the strike. A crack echoed with the hit. The handle snapped, the end landing close to her head. Emma ducked and looked up again just in time to see the man and Thayne collide.

"No," Emma cried out when the man locked his hands around Thayne's neck.

Thayne forced his arms up breaking the hold, then pulled his arm back and smashed his fist into the man's face over and over again. The man dropped to the ground and fell forward, face down.

Thayne dropped his hands to his knees, hunched over, drawing in gulps of air for a minute before staggering toward her. Emma pushed up to reach for him.

"Come on." He grabbed her hand pulling her across the sand. A motor fired up as they reached the dock. He hauled her to a smaller speed boat with a man at the wheel. The man turned and reached a hand out to her. When Thayne didn't appear worried, she took it and stepped on board, dropping into a seat. Thayne released the front line then jumped on.

"Go!" Thayne pulled her up, sat in the seat and lowered her into his lap as they backed away from the dock. Emma wrapped her arms around his neck. He buried his face in her hair, holding her to him.

The man gunned the engine and they shot forward, racing over the water.

Chapter Twelve

He was alive. Tears burned Emma's eyes. She had almost been afraid to truly hope.

Thayne hugged her tight, his breath stirring on her neck. His lips brush over the tender skin, and Emma went weak against him. She'd thought she'd lost him, but he was real, solid in her arms.

The vision of him lying on the ground at the bottom of the rocks burst back into her mind. She tightened her hold. His arms answered squeezing down on her. Another kiss touched her neck then moved up to her chin. Thayne tipped his head back and stared at her a second before running a hand up into her hair.

"I was afraid I'd lost you." He tilted her head down to meet his lips. His kiss alternated between devouring her and savoring.

Her heart soared with each sensation.

When he broke the kiss, he wrapped his arms around her, burying his head into her neck once more.

"Thayne." The man driving the boat called out his name. "I think we have company."

Thayne jerked up his head, twisting in the seat. Emma had a good view of boat lights bobbing on the water behind them. It was coming fast.

"I thought you disabled it," Thayne said, sliding her off his lap onto the seat so he could shift more fully around.

"I did. I cut the wires to the ignition."

Emma saw Thayne flinch, but he didn't comment, instead he said, "Emma, this is James." His attention remained behind them. "They're gaining. Go faster."

"I'm full open now. They have a lot more power with the three engines."

"Do you have a gun?"

"Just a spear gun and flares." The man shouted back.

"Lose them."

Unfortunately, they were on open water. There was nowhere to hide. They whipped by one boat drifting out there, but it wasn't big enough to give them any cover. Emma figured it was at least two miles to the harbor. She glanced back at the boat. It had closed half the distance.

"Where's the flares?" Thayne yelled.

"The side, behind me," James called back.

Thayne gripped the back of James' seat and crouched as he edged across the boat. They hit a wave that almost jerked him from his feet. Emma caught her breath until Thayne dropped onto the bench seat. He reached in and pulled out a case.

She took it when he extended it toward her. He reached back in the cubby hole and pulled out a sheathed diver's knife and a spear-gun.

Emma didn't want to think how close the attackers would have to be for the knife or the spear-gun to be of any use. Thayne strapped the knife to his calf before he moved back over to her, wedging onto the seat. He handed her the spear gun and took the case.

Emma had never shot a flare gun before but knew the basics to it. She watched as Thayne loaded the cartridge into it. He glanced back. She followed his gaze. The other boat was only about seventy to a hundred feet behind.

"Get down," he ordered.

Emma didn't argue. She slid off the seat to the floor. "Do you think they have a gun?"

He didn't take his eyes off the other boat. "I'm not

going to chance it." He held the gun low behind the seat, locked in both hands.

A bright beam of light swung across the boat, highlighting him. James jerked the wheel to the side just as three shots rang out.

"I guess that answers that." There was a hint of mirth in Thayne's voice. "Bad guys always get the toys. Bring us around." He sharpened the end words and two more shots punctuated it. One hit the side of the boat with a dull thud. James whipped the boat around the other way almost dumping Thayne off the seat. He steadied himself then in a smooth motion that defied the rough ride, brought the flare gun up and fired. There was a flash.

Emma caught a stream of light and smoke as it zipped toward the other boat. The boat angled away at the last instant, and the flare shot past, dipped into the water and died out.

They gained a little more space but a second later the chase was back on.

Thayne dug in the case for another flare. The engines of the other boat roared as it closed in on them again. Another volley of shots rang out peppering the side of the boat before James could angle away. The larger boat cut after them as Thayne snapped the gun closed. He prepped then rose.

There was another burst as the flare erupted from the gun heading right toward the other boat. They tried to turn away but this time there wasn't enough distance between them. The flare hit the front of the boat and burst. The boat jerked around wildly as the driver lost control.

James straightened out their craft and headed toward the harbor.

"Stay down," Thayne said when she started to rise. She got a glimpse of smoke and flames rising up behind them.

"Do you think it killed them?" She couldn't help asking, not really sure what she hoped.

"No, at least two jumped overboard. When the driver cut the engines and turned, it sent a wake over the front, extinguishing most of the flames. I just hope we did enough damage they won't be after us again."

"I say we don't wait around to find out," Emma exclaimed.

"Smart lady," James spoke up.

Thayne settled next to Emma, cuddling her into his side and tried to relax. Now having time to catch his breath and think, he hurt like crazy. But with Emma next to him he didn't care. He had her – that was all that mattered. Her arms slipped over his chest. She rested her head on his shoulder.

Thayne turned to press a kiss on her forehead. "Are you all right?"

"Just tired. I thought I'd lost you."

He detected a hitch in her voice and understood the feeling well. "I'm not letting you get away that easy." He felt her burrow into him.

She jerked back. "Your side!"

"It's fine." He tightened his hold.

They both fell silent as the boat skimmed over the water. A few minutes later, James slowed and wove his way into shore. Once docked, they got into James's late model sedan, and headed to the other side of the island to a private resort.

James went in and secured the room while Emma dozed against Thayne's shoulder.

The sun was starting to lighten the sky when they walked into their room. Thayne did a quick sweep of the suite. There was only one bedroom, but the living room couch had a pull out. They were on the second floor with a patio that looked out on the golf course and a small pond. He studied the area thoroughly before returning to the door where Emma waited with James.

"Thank you." Thayne reached out and shook the man's

hand.

"No problem. You've added some excitement to my life. By the way, here's the new passport for Emma."

"New passport?" Emma asked.

Thayne reached out accepting the small blue booklet.

James slipped out the door.

Thayne turned the lock before opening the passport. First, he was greeted with several colorful stamps listing a couple locations and showed her coming in from Malaysia. He flipped through pages until coming to the photo of her. They'd modified and used one of the pictures taken with him on the island. She was beautiful, but what caught his attention was the name they'd given her, though he wasn't really surprised.

She leaned into him. "That's me."

He held it out to her. "Hello, Mrs. Emma Rees." He leaned down and kissed her.

Unfortunately, she was more focused on the passport. "How?" She looked up at him.

"Connections. Don't worry. It will go through."

Emma bit the edge of her lip and looked at him as if she was going to ask more questions, then just shook her head. "Why Rees?"

"Probably because that's my last name."

A shadow seemed to wash over her.

Thayne felt a stab of unease. "You don't like it?"

She blinked slightly dazed. "Oh, no, that's not it. Is that your real name?"

His concern spiked. "Yes." He drew the word out as he studied her, trying to figure out what she was thinking. "Emma?"

She blinked and looked up at him. "I just realized. I agreed to marry you, and I didn't even know your last name." Her right hand came up to cover her mouth.

Thayne looked at her just as stunned by the realization. He started to speak but didn't know what to say. He cleared his throat. "Well," he finally got out, "as long as you know I love you."

Her eyes grew bright. Suddenly, her hand dropped. She was smiling then let out a little laugh. She threw her arms around his neck. "I do know. And, I love you, too." She went up on her toes and kissed him.

Thayne's world righted, though exhaustion was starting to take over again. Still, he relished the feel of her. His heart raced. It took all his strength to end the kiss, tilting his head back. Her face glowed. He wanted to continue to kiss her, but eased back further.

Light hit her face as it was tilted up to him. For the first time, he noticed traces of dried blood from a small cut just below her hairline and a shadow on her chin. The bruise wasn't dark or overly large but there was no missing it.

"They hurt you." Cold anger ran through him. He raised his hand to her chin, tilting it up gently so he could get a better look.

She touched her jaw. "It's all right. Just a bit sore."

He stiffened. Fury built in him.

Emma must've picked up on it. "Thayne," she said soothingly and ran her hand over his arm. "I'm all right."

After a moment, the tightness eased inside him. "I'm sorry sweetheart. Did they hurt you anywhere else?" He let his gaze run over her, inspecting her for any signs of pain or injury. He didn't see any.

"Again, I'm fine. I have a few scrapes and bruises. That's all, but we better check your side."

"I'm…" He started to protest, but broke off when one eyebrow kicked up as she stared at him. He lowered his backpack strap from his shoulder, released her and stepped to the table lowering the pack down. He unzipped it and took out a waterproof case and handed it to her. Wordlessly, she opened it while he pulled off his shirt.

She let out a small cry at the sight of the wound. He

looked down. Blood had pooled in the bandages, visible through the clear seal. There were also several rather large bruises on his chest. His only consolation was the other guys would've had just as much damage and they didn't have Emma tending them.

"It's not as bad as it looks," he said trying to relieve her mind.

She pushed him down in a chair. Her hand trembled as she ran it over his skin, taking stock. Her touch was gentle as she came in contact where there was some bruising on his ribs. Still, despite trying not to, he flinched.

"Sorry," she said, glancing up to meet his eyes. "I don't think they're broke. You'd have to have an x-rayed to know for sure though.

He placed his hand over the area and felt, swallowing back a groan of pain. "I don't think they are. Just bruised."

"Have you had broken ribs before?" There was hesitation in her voice as she asked the question.

"Yes," he answered honestly.

She raised her hand to the scar of his shoulder.

"I was shot," he said to her unasked question. He caught her hands in one hand, the other he raised to her cheek, cupping the soft skin, bringing her to meet his gaze. "Emma, when I told you I was changing jobs, I was telling the truth. This is my last job. I have already handed in my resignation. I plan to spend the rest of my life being a boring engineer, happily married to you, and maybe a scout master."

"Something tells me you will never be boring, but I hope you will be happy."

He smiled. "That I think is assured."

"You know we really don't know anything about each other."

"Are you trying to tell me you have some very annoying habits?"

"Me? I was wondering about you." A twinkle sparkled

in her eyes that he found very appealing.

"Well, let's see. I am known to leave gadgets I'm working on around the house, but I do usually put my tools away. I'm told I'm a Type A, dominant personality. I'm not sure exactly what that means, but I like to be in charge."

She laughed. "Exactly. I don't know an engineer that isn't." She removed the bandage and started to clean the area.

"I'm good at fixing things around the house and cars."

"That's handy."

"What about you?" he asked more to keep her mind from dwelling on what she was doing, though she didn't seem the least bit squeamish about the blood.

"I am not dominant. I've always been called a peacemaker. I try to fix things, as in people. I'm also artistic."

"Really?"

"Yes, I paint. You know this really should be stitched up."

He looked down at his side. She'd done an excellent job cleaning it. The bleeding had stopped, but she was right. It needed to be closed. "There's some medical glue in there." He reached into the first aid kit and found it.

Her eyebrow arched and lips tightened.

"I can do it," he assured her, figuring her nerves had been stretched enough for one night.

She reached out and took the small tube from him before he could open it. Her hands were steady, but he saw her take a deep breath before she broke the seal on the tube. She worked methodically, a lot more gentle than he and a lot of doctors would have been. He was impressed. "You're pretty good at this."

She shrugged. "Between sports and my brother and his friends, I got used to patching them up."

"You also don't seem to panic easily."

"I've had my moments the last couple days."

Thayne noticed a shiver run over her. He reached out and took the tube she'd just closed and put it on the table. Wrapping his arms around her waist, he urged her down onto his lap. Her arms slipped around his neck as he pulled her in.

"I was really afraid I'd lost you today," she whispered, laying her head on his shoulder.

"I know the feeling." He turned his head to press a kiss to her forehead. She raised her mouth to meet his. He took the offering, enjoying the feel of her. His heart was pounding when they broke apart, the pain in his side was totally forgotten.

He wanted to lift her in his arms and carry her to the bedroom. Not that he had the strength to do it. He was exhausted and needed rest but more importantly, it wasn't time yet. *But soon*, he promised himself. He kissed her again. *Very soon.* "Why don't you go in and get some sleep? I'll take the couch out here." He eased her off his lap.

"The couch isn't big enough for you," she objected.

"Emma," he said simply. He could tell she wanted to argue, but she nodded and went to the other room. A second later, Thayne heard the shower come on.

He waited a minute then stood. His body ached in protest at the movement. His shirt was a bloody mess on the floor and his shorts weren't in much better shape. He reached in the back pack and pulled out a bag with a fresh T-shirt and a pair of shorts. It was all they had until they could buy some clothes. James would see to it that their luggage was retrieved and taken to the airport but couldn't risk bringing it to them now.

He walked into the bedroom and laid the T-shirt out on the bed for Emma before walking back to the table. He checked the cut on his side. She had done a great job tending it. Still, it hurt like crazy. He put on another water proof bandage then looked at the time and decided it was safe to take a couple more pain pills and an antibiotic. Infection still would be his biggest worry, though they should be home in seventy-two hours. It seemed like a long time and yet no time at all. It hit him that, that was about how long he'd known Emma.

Thayne shook his head. So much had happened, but even with the danger they were in, he truly couldn't regret having Emma here.

The water stopped. Thayne heard her leave the bathroom and waited a few minutes before going to the bedroom door. When he tapped, there was no answer. He cracked open the door. Emma had left the light on in the bathroom, probably for him and it spilled out to illuminate her on the bed. She was wearing his T-shirt, curled on her side, already asleep.

The sight of her brought a smile to his lips. Thayne stood, staring down at her. She was so pretty. He wanted a lifetime of watching her. With her high cheek bones, he bet she was one of those women who would age beautifully. He forced himself to turn away.

The shower felt wonderful. He stayed under the spray letting it pound out his sore muscles until he found himself starting to fall asleep. He felt beat but alive again as he dried off and pulled on his shorts.

His intention was to make it quickly through the bedroom but made the mistake of looking at Emma again. Unable to stop himself, he took a step to the bed. More than anything, he wanted to stretch out beside her and just hold her. Instead, he leaned down and brushed his lips over her cheek.

She sighed in her sleep.

Thayne forced himself away, but his thoughts remained on her as he settled on the couch and let exhaustion take him.

Chapter Thirteen

Emma woke to another strange room, but the memories came back so fast she didn't have time to be scared. She knew Thayne was just on the other side of the wall. She slipped from the bed and padded to the bedroom door. It was cracked open. Emma opened it farther and peeked into the living room.

It was dark but for the glow that came around the curtains. Still there was enough light to see Thayne plainly on the bed. He had kicked the blanket off his legs and it only covered half his torso, which was bare. She could just make out he was wearing a pair of shorts.

She stepped closer. He looked so peaceful. Morning growth of a beard shadowed his face. Her fingers itched to touch him but she didn't. Not wanting to wake him. His body needed rest to heal.

She shuddered at the thought of the knife wound. It wasn't the first one he'd received, he'd also been shot. Her heart hurt at the thought of him injured. She wondered how it happened, where he'd been, who took care of him. Something told her he'd been alone – that he'd been alone for a long time.

She knew how that felt. She'd been alone a long time, too. Often, she felt she was letting life slip by. But, every time she'd looked at a man, she'd known he wasn't the right one. When she looked at Thayne, it was just the opposite. He was the one.

Emma forced herself to leave him sleeping and went back to the bathroom. She'd rinsed out clothes the night before and surprisingly, despite the humidity, they were dry. She glanced at the clock by the bed. It was almost noon. That explained it and no wonder she was starving. She changed quickly then found the room service menu and ordered a large breakfast for both of them. While waiting, she opened the bedroom curtains and gazed out at the beautiful scene.

Bright orange bird of paradise reached up to the railing along with bamboo. She unlatched the sliding glass door and stepped out onto the balcony. Warmth, humidity and the smell of plumeria greeted her. She sighed, taking it in. After all that happened the night before, she found herself another day in paradise.

Emma became aware of someone moving behind her but felt no fear as arms slid around her waist. She settled back against Thayne, laying her arms over his. He kissed her neck, exciting a shiver from her. He seemed to like to kiss her neck, and she loved it. She never knew she was so sensitive there. "It's beautiful out here," she said.

"Yes. How are you this morning?"

She sighed. "Good. How is your side?"

"Not bad, a little sore."

She turned, wrapping her arms up around his neck. "I ordered room service. It should be here soon."

"Good, I'm starving." He leaned down as she stretched up to kiss him.

Emma buried her fingers in the short hair at the base of his neck. She liked his hair. He growled as she stroked his neck.

"That feels so good," he said between kisses.

Emma was about to agree when there was a knock on the door.

"That will be room service." She started to step past him.

"Stay in the bedroom." He caught her hand holding her back, then went to answer the door.

She waited for him to call her out. Instead, a second after she heard the door close, he stepped into the bedroom carrying a large tray laden with covered dishes.

"I thought we'd eat out here." He moved past her to the balcony, setting the tray on the table. "I like how you order breakfast," he said as he uncovered dishes.

"I thought you'd need calories to get your strength up."

"Got that right." He held out a chair for her.

They ate ravenously the first few minutes until they'd appeased their hunger enough to slow enough to talk.

"According to the brochure," Thayne opened to the map to show her, "there's a little shopping village here in the resort. We can get some clothes there. There should also be huts on the beach. Want to take a walk after we finish eating?"

"Sure." Emma was excited to go look around. She'd been afraid Thayne would insist they spend the whole time in the room, which wouldn't have been bad since she was with him, but she could feel tension rising between them.

It wasn't a bad kind of tension, she thought trying not to stare at his chest. Thayne had a great chest. She wanted to run her hands over it, which, after catching some of the heated looks he gave her wouldn't be fair to him or her. So she'd rather go look around the resort instead of go crazy.

⊙ൠ

Emma sighed at the pure beauty of the plumeria tree-lined path they walked on. The scent of flowers was intoxicating. Thayne took her hand, interlocking their fingers. He stopped her. Reaching up, he picked one of the white blossoms and tucked it above her ear.

"I've fallen in love with these," Emma said taking in the sweet fragrance.

"We'll have to plant one in our yard. I know just the spot, right off the deck, outside our bedroom." His eyes picked up a gleam. He went on to tell her about his house that was not far off the beach. "If you don't like it, we can always move, but it shouldn't be far for you to drive to work." he added.

"It sounds lovely."

"Well, actually I don't have much furniture. I only bought the house a couple years ago because I hated the feel of coming home to the commotion that always seemed to be around my apartment. I just wanted a place to relax." He glanced at her as if wondering how she would take what he said.

"I can understand that."

"I have a bedroom set, leather couch, recliner, and a TV."

"Big screen," she guessed.

"Of course." He squeezed her hand.

Emma smiled and leaned into him.

"I do have bar stools at the kitchen counter. That's where I usually eat or out on the patio. I have a nice patio set and grill out there. Basically, what I'm saying is you can do whatever you want with the place."

"Big pink flowers everywhere."

He looked pained. "Please tell me you're teasing."

She laughed. "I am. How about we look for stuff together?"

"I can go for that."

They reached the shopping area. There was a small grocery store, several souvenir and clothing shops, a jewelry store, tailor, leather shop and bakery. Instead of splitting up, Thayne insisted on staying with her.

Emma found it fun having his opinion. Because of him, beside a couple shirts, some baggie Thai pants like she'd been tempted by several days earlier, she ended up with another new swimsuit, this one a royal blue, and a flowing white dress that hugged her waist and flowed around her calves. She also got white high-heeled sandals to go with the dress and a pair of leather casual flats that were extremely comfortable and reasonably priced. Thayne got leather loafers, two pairs of pants, two button-up shirts, a T-shirt and swimsuit.

"I've sure been hard on luggage here," Emma commented when they stepped into the shop to look at bags.

"Don't worry. James will see that our luggage is delivered to the airport. It will get home with us."

"So I don't have to start shopping for souvenirs all over again?"

"Not unless you see something you like." Thayne picked out a duffle bag and started to bargain with the shopkeeper until he got the price he wanted, which was probably a couple dollars more than he could have gotten it in town but it was still a great price. Thayne arranged to have everything delivered to their room.

They stepped out onto the sidewalk as rain started to come down. Hand in hand, they made a dash for the bakery, getting in just before a lot of the other shoppers with the same idea. They ordered pastries then sat down by one of the big glass windows to watch the rain pour down.

"It's amazing that it was blue skies a few minutes ago." Emma watched the torrent.

"And it will be again in an hour," Thayne said in way of agreement. "If you want, we can get a shuttle back or we can wait and walk?"

"Let's wait. Maybe walk on the beach."

"We do that and we'll walk by the wedding chapel." His eyes grew intense as he looked at her. "But we need to make one more stop before we leave here. How's your chocolate thing?" He changed the subject.

"Incredible. Want a bite?"

He leaned forward and let her feed him. His gaze caught and held hers. Emma felt her lungs tighten. Her heart raced. His lips curved up, as if he knew his effect on her.

"Mmm," he let the sound of appreciation rumble in his throat. "You taste better." He stretched across the table and kissed her as if to prove it.

When he settled back a second later, the rain had eased slightly. By the time they finished the last few bites of their pastries, the rain was just a light drizzle.

"Ready to go?" Thayne stood and reached out his hand.

Emma took it, but as she stood, he released her hand to slide his arm around her waist. "You fit in nice against me," he whispered in her ear and once again her pulse leapt.

Emma wondered if she would ever be able to breathe normally around him. Thayne packed some punch. She lost her breath again when he drew her into the jewelry store. Unlike the souvenir shops, this one had high-end jewelry.

"All our diamonds and gem stones are a hundred percent certified and guaranteed," the man at the counter assured them a minute later as Thayne seated her in front of a case with wedding rings in it.

"See anything you like?" Thayne asked.

Shocked, Emma could only stare down at the rings. "I don't know. They're all beautiful."

"Let's see if we can narrow it down. Do you like a lot of little diamonds around the main stone?"

Emma looked at the section he pointed. "Not really."

"Good, I can't say that appeals to me, but I'm a guy. I kind of like that." He pointed to a solitaire, in which the white gold came up and wrapped around a round cut diamond.

"That's beautiful." She was about to say it was probably very expensive, but was too late as Thayne was already having the man bring it out.

Thayne lifted her hand and slid the ring on her finger. "What do you think?"

Emma could do nothing but stare. She'd never seen a ring so beautiful. It truly shone like a star snatched from the night sky. She was still staring at it when she heard Thayne ask for a jeweler's loop. She watched in fascination as he raised her hand and studied the diamond, tilting her hand back and forth.

"Do you like it?" He shifted his gaze from it to her.

"It's gorgeous, but I don't need anything so ... extravagant."

Thayne looked at the tag then gave a lower price. The man looked at him a moment then nodded, not even countering back. Emma was surprised, not because of him bargaining, that was what you did for everything there. What surprised her was that Thayne won his price so fast.

Emma looked down at the ring on her finger and realized the amazing ring was there to stay. Her heart fluttered. She couldn't believe it.

"Do you like it?" Thayne repeated, picking up her hand. He raised it to his lips.

"Yes." She managed to get the word out, and then got lost at the intensity in his eyes, no less striking than the ring.

"Good. Let's see what we can find for me."

With effort, Emma pulled her gaze from him and studied the case of men's rings.

"What do you like?" she asked.

"I'm actually kind of partial to the titanium. It's durable, and I work with my hands a lot."

Emma turned her attention to the titanium rings, settling on one that had beveled edges and small diamond chips inlaid at intervals around the ring. "What do you think of that?"

The man pulled it out of the case as soon as she pointed to it. Thayne took it and slipped it on. "I like it." Thayne said. "The fit is good." He flexed his fingers. "Yes."

He pulled the ring off and put it in the box and started the bargaining process again. Thayne handed over his credit card, and then signed the receipt after checking the total.

"I think I was supposed to buy your ring," she said as they walked out of the store.

He shrugged. "It didn't make sense not to run them together."

She thought about him checking it with the jeweler loop. "Do you know much about diamonds?"

"A little. I worked on an assignment that dealt with them. I had to learn a little. I know how to spot a fake and tell a good quality, cut, and clarity. And this," He caught her hand bringing it to his lips. "I'm pleased to say, is a very nice stone."

"All I know it's very beautiful. Bigger than I would've ever planned on."

"I'm thinking of it as an investment. I plan on it being there for a very long time." He kissed her knuckles again." He met her gaze, growing very serious. "Emma, I know I'm hurrying you, but I love you and wanted my ring there."

"Well, since my passport says we're married," she fought the smile that slipped free anyway, "that means you have to wear yours on the way home, too."

"Not a bad idea. In fact, I'm getting some thoughts on that. Come here." He kissed her then led her down the path to the beach.

The beach, like everything else, was beautiful and far less crowded than where she'd stayed before. They took a moment to sit in the lounge chairs that a boy from the hotel staff hurried to wipe off for them. The waves rolled in kissing the sand. Everything smelled clean and fresh. It seemed hard to believe that about twelve hours earlier she'd been frightened for her and Thayne's life.

Emma dozed off aware of Thayne talking on the

phone. Contentment hummed through her body when the lounge she was sitting on shifted and she felt a light tickle on her neck. She opened her eyes. The sun was blocked out again, but not by clouds.

Blue eyes framed with long dark lashes sparkled down at her. "Wake up, sleeping beauty." He kissed her lightly. "Let's head back to the room, and you can take a nap there."

Emma didn't want to move but let him pull her up. He held her hand until they were off the sand and on the path then he wrapped his arms around her.

"I should let my parents know I'm going to be late getting home. Originally I was to board the plane today."

He pulled out his phone then glanced at his watch. "Actually, why don't you wait until this evening? It's the middle of the night right now."

"All right." They took the path that led past one of the buildings to a bridge over a pool, then curved out around the pond. Just off the trail in front of them sat a large white building with the distinct Asian flare sitting on pillars over the water. Water lilies drifted around it. Flowers lined the bridge and the open-sided structure. Filmy white curtains billowed in the light breeze.

Thayne guided her to it.

"Oh, this is beautiful." Emma released his hand as they entered. Hands on the railing, she looked out over the water. Thayne came up behind her, placing a hand on either side of her, pressing his lips to her neck. She shivered in reaction.

He seemed to have an insatiable need to kiss her, not that she was going to complain, but her nerve endings were going haywire. She yearned to turn and kiss him back, but was afraid that if she did, she wouldn't want to stop.

"What..." She stopped to swallow back a moan that almost slipped free before she started again, "What is this place?" She leaned back into him.

"The wedding chapel," he whispered the words against her neck.

"Yes." She groaned.

"That's almost the word that's to be said here." He wrapped his arms around her. "The word I want to hear you say."

"Thayne?"

He broke off kissing her and turned her in his arms. Kneeling down, he looked up. "Emma, will you marry me?"

Chapter Fourteen

Thayne's gaze was so intent there was no mistaking the love and sincerity in the words.

Joy burst within Emma. "Yes," she whispered the word again. Her lips trembled.

"I mean here, today. In two hours."

"Thayne?"

"I'm not saying we have to consummate it tonight, but I want you to have my name, besides just on your passport."

She felt a wave of fear, not of him but for him. He was worried. "What's wrong?"

"Nothing that I know of, but I'd feel better if we were married. My company would have more pull if anything happened, that's all. Mainly, I want you to be mine. Would you marry me here? Sorry, I was going to be romantic. I guess I kind of botched it. When we get home we can have another ceremony with all your family and friends, but for now—"

"Yes." She cut him off. "If you're certain."

He closed his eyes then opened them. Relief was evident on his face. "I am."

CBEO

Two hours later, Emma and Thayne stood almost in the exact same spot, this time in front of a preacher. Emma wore the flowing dress she'd bought earlier. Thayne had disappeared while she was in the shower. When he returned to escort her to the wedding chapel he wore a light gray suit and a bright yellow tie that match the throats on the bouquet of plumeria blossoms he held out to her.

James and a woman from the US Consulate, who had delivered their paper work for the marriage, stood as witnesses. Thayne didn't say how he pulled that feat off, and Emma wasn't worried about it. All her thoughts were on the handsome man that had just pledged to love her forever. Thayne's eyes echoed the words, vowing them with his soul.

"Do you take this man?"

Emma realized the preacher was repeating the words to her. "Oh, yes, I do."

Thayne smiled at her answer. His head was already dipping when the man announced them as husband and wife and said, "You may now kiss your bride." The kiss was long and deep, full of promise for years to come. Emma gave herself over to the kiss. Thayne accepted her and gave back of himself.

The camera in James's hands whirled as he took photos.

When Thayne eased back, Emma had to hold on to him just to remain upright. Her legs trembled. She caught hold of his waist to steady herself. She felt no risk of falling as Thayne wrapped his arm around her, holding her to him. He turned her to face James so he could get more shots of them.

The woman from the consulate dabbed at her eyes. "Oh, that was beautiful."

"I guess you need us to sign some papers," Thayne said, his voice low and husky that sent tremors off in Emma's stomach.

"Yes, please. I have to get back." She picked up the paperwork and stepped toward them to have them sign. "I've never had the chance to do anything like this before. I must say you made my week."

After Emma signed the document, the woman leaned in and kissed her on the cheek. "Congratulation and good luck."

"Thank you. I appreciate you taking the time to come do this, especially, on such short notice." Emma meant every word.

"It was my pleasure. Though, you must have some high-up friends to get my boss to process the paperwork so fast," the woman smiled as she put the documents in her briefcase.

Emma glanced at Thayne. He just shrugged. "Thank you," he said to the woman.

The preacher shook their hands and wished them good fortune on their marriage.

James was the last to step up. "I want a chance to kiss the bride." He edged Thayne aside to kiss Emma on the cheek. "Such a beautiful bride. Are you sure you want this man? He's nothing but trouble."

Emma laughed. "I'm sure." Her heart felt like it would overflow with joy.

James looked over at Thayne. "Actually, come to think about it. She's the one who's always in trouble. I could take her off your hands." At the look Thayne gave him, he pulled back. "Second thought, no." James glanced back over at her. "He gets too aggressive where you're involved."

"Protective," Thayne growled.

James laughed. "I'll send the photos to your e-mail."

"Thank you." Thayne said, shaking the man's hand.

"I'll be here tomorrow to take you to the airport. Your baggage has already been picked up and will be delivered directly there tomorrow morning. I'd stay away from it. Just in case." The man shrugged

Thayne nodded.

Emma stepped forward, placing another kiss on the man's cheek. "Thank you," she said softly.

He bowed to her then left, leaving them standing there alone. Thayne's arm tightened around her waist, pulling her back into him. Emma went willingly, tilting her face up to meet his lips. She groaned as he took command of the kiss. Heat seared her as he lifted his gaze to stare at her.

"You are so beautiful," he breathed out. "Mrs. Rees." His voice seemed to caress the name. He touched the flower in her hair.

A look that Emma felt was regret came over him though he continued to gaze at her. "What do you say about going to eat at one of the places on the beach? We can watch the sunset. I have a table reserved for us."

Her nerves were a flutter. Emma wanted to say she would rather go back to their room and eat in private. Instead, she nodded remembering he'd said. *"We don't have to consummate the wedding until after we get home."* Did that mean he wasn't planning on making love to her tonight?

Yes. She felt tension in his body. That was exactly what he meant. But, did it also mean he didn't want her at all? She shook her head at the idea. He kissed her continually and was forever touching her. He made her feel desirable. He was the one that pressed them to get married here, but he'd also said he'd wanted it in case something happened. Did he only marry her, pay attention to her, to keep her in line so he could protect her?

Her heart screamed, "No!" at the idea, but what did she know of men. After the last time she thought that she understood a man's attention and failed so miserably she'd always kept herself away from relationships. Now, she'd fallen in four days. One day really, she had fallen in love with Thayne in one day.

His fingers skimmed over her waist as he slid his arm around her to draw her out of the chapel. She glanced back over her shoulder. He stopped and turned her back.

"So beautiful," she whispered.

"I tend to be extremely practical."

She looked up at him.

"But, I would say it was the perfect place." He framed her face, and all the doubts she'd been experiencing wafted away. Thayne wanted her. He loved her. Once again, fire burned in his eyes, but he gave her only one long, solitary kiss before directed her along the path in the opposite direction of the room.

At the beach, he knelt and undid her sandals. His hands sliding lightly over her calves, making her legs go weak again as he removed them.

He picked up her shoes and carried them in one hand, her hand held firmly in his other. At the restaurant they were led to a table just off the sand. Candles flickered, already lit, though the sun hadn't yet started to dip into the sea. Pinks and oranges were just starting to tint the sky. After taking their orders and filling their glasses, they were left alone.

"Tomorrow afternoon we will head home." He looked at her then glanced out over the water. "You wanted to call your parents." He handed her his phone continuing to gaze at the waves.

Emma punched in the number and listened to it ring. Unfortunately, the call went directly to the answering machine.

"Hi," she said. "Wanted to let you know, I will be coming in on a different flight a day later. I'm coming into San Diego. Don't worry, everything is all right. I have a ride, so don't worry about meeting me. I'll probably see you Sunday, but I'll call and let you know when I arrive." She looked across the table at Thayne watching her. "I have a surprise for you. Love you. Bye."

The intensity in his eyes burned hot. They took her breath. She felt like he wanted to devour her.

⋐⋑

Thayne wanted Emma like he'd never wanted

anything. *His wife.* The words thundered over and over again in his mind. He promised he would wait. Give her more time, but from the moment the preacher had pronounced them one, he wanted to be one with her.

He wondered if he should call the airport and see if he could get a flight out now. Then he'd have to behave. Keep his hands off her. He wanted his hands on her. He tried to keep them to himself, but he had this insistent need to touch her. More than anything, he wanted to take her in his arms and make love to her.

His wife. He groaned at the thought. *His sweet innocent Emma.* Just the touch of her fingers brushing his when he handed her his phone was like connecting to a live wire. He couldn't touch her again. He made the mistake of looking across the table at her. The warm hues of the sun blazed over her. Her hair shimmered golden. Her blue eyes were depths he wanted to get lost in. *Patience. I promised.*

He was to the point of snapping when, fortunately, their dinner arrived. The shrimp, vegetables and rice was fabulous. Thayne ate with gusto, trying to pay attention to his plate but was aware of every move Emma made. He never knew eating could be so enticing. As good as the food was, he wanted to taste her more. Just one kiss, would be enough. The thought ran through his mind and he knew it was a lie. He wanted all of her.

The server approached their table asking again if they wanted something other than water to drink. "I better not," he declined.

When Emma shook her head the soft mass of her hair picked up the colors of the setting sun and reflected it back. He was in trouble. He needed to request another suite. There was no way he could remain with Emma and stay honorable. *She was his wife.*

The light hit the diamond on her finger. Emma tilted her hand up looking at the ring. He glanced at the ring she'd placed on his finger. It felt surprisingly good there.

Married. They were married.

He looked at Emma. She still stared at her ring. "I can't believe it. It feels like a dream," she whispered.

Thayne closed his fingers over hers, raising their hand so their rings showed side-by-side. She met his gaze.

"Ready to go?" He couldn't believe he'd asked the question. It would be better if they remained around people, but she was already nodding.

He released her hand long enough to pull out his wallet and drop some money on the table. Then he had her hand firmly back in his.

They stepped onto the sand as the sun sank into the water, filling the sky with color. He led her out where the waves rushed up to meet them.

"Our last sunset here," she said softly, looking out over the water.

Unable to stop himself, Thayne wrapped his arms around her pulling her back into him. He kissed her neck, feeling the shiver that ran through her. His body shuddered in answer.

"I'll bring you back. What do you think, for our twentieth anniversary?"

She sighed. "Yes."

He needed to let go of her. Still, it took a full minute to force his arms open. As soon as he did, she turned to him looking like an innocent offering. He bit back the groan that rumbled up inside him.

That was just what she was – an innocent that got caught in a world of mess because of him. He was responsible to get her out. He couldn't take advantage of her. She needed more time to work out her true feelings.

"Thayne."

"We better start back." He stepped farther away so he didn't reach for her again. He held her shoes in the hand between them for an excuse not to touch her. She fell silent as they walked. He wondered what she was thinking, but didn't dare risk himself to ask.

The balmy night air kissed their skin as they walked along the lit path. The pool was empty, the whole resort peaceful. They skirted around the deserted poolside bar area and up over the bridge that spanned the pool. Instead of taking the path that circled around the pond to the wedding chapel, they stayed straight, taking a more direct route serenaded by frogs and bugs.

Thayne heard Emma sigh beside him. His body hummed in answer. Unable to resist, he glanced at her. He tried to force his eyes away but they went right back. *His wife.* The words came again to him driven by another surge of hunger for her.

It was going to be a long twenty-four hours until they got on the plane. He pushed back his need. What was he thinking? Until she was his, it would be interminable. *His wife.* This time the words shouted in his mind. How would he survive keeping his promise of waiting? He wanted her so much.

Moonlight bathed her as she stopped along the path, looking out over the water at the small, glowing white chapel just across from them. "It was a perfect place to get married," she whispered.

He stopped behind her and shoved his hands into his pockets. "I'm sorry your family wasn't there."

"It's all right," she said smoothly.

The way she sounded, Thayne could almost believe it was true, that it hadn't mattered to her.

"When would you like to be married in the states?" *Please don't wait too long.* He almost pleaded aloud.

She shrugged. "It doesn't matter."

A surge of panic washed over him. Was she saying she really didn't want to marry him? Before he could form words to ask, she turned to him.

"Thayne, about our marriage here…"

Cold speared in his heart. *She didn't want it, didn't*

want him. He forced his gaze away not wanting to see the truth in her eyes − that she didn't love him. Her hand touched his face to turn it back to her. He tried to resist, but couldn't.

Her eyes were as captivating as the night around them, but mostly he thought they were filled with love. He didn't think more, just dipped his head and kissed her.

She whimpered and pressed closer.

Abruptly he ripped away, putting several feet between them. He had to stop tormenting himself. "I'm sorry. I promised." He got the words out. "I'll get another room." He tried to breathe deeply to calm himself but all it did was pull in her alluring fragrance.

"Thayne." There was a quiver in her voice when she said his name.

He figured he'd startled her.

"I want to make love with you." Her words were so soft, it took him a second to realize she'd really said the words, and they weren't just his imagination.

He felt her fingers on his arm, branding his soul. Light sparkled from the ring he'd put there. *His wife.* "Emma, I'll wait," he didn't know how he said the words.

"I know, but I don't want you to." For as smooth and firm as her words were, there was a timorous quality to her.

"When we get home, you might decide what happened here was a ... was all just being here. If we don't ... it would be simple to get an annulment." The words hurt to say. He looked up at her.

"I'm not going to stop loving you. I ..." She glanced away. "If you..."

Thayne caught her to him. "I love you." He kissed her, then buried his face into her hair.

"Then, please." She wrapped her arms around his neck.

Thayne's heart jumped then soared. He ran kisses along her neck, over her chin up to her lips. She let out a soft cry. He pulled back to look down at her. Her eyes had closed. When they floated open, he saw all he needed. Emma was his.

Thayne shifted an arm from around her back to under her legs and lifted her into his arms. She gasped lightly, tightening her arms around his neck but didn't protest as he started once more down the sidewalk in a ground-eating stride. A security guard at the end of the path made no comment as they passed by.

Thayne crossed the driveway to their building and took the stairs up not willing to wait for the elevator. Outside their suite, he had to put her down to reach the room keycard, but as soon as the green light flicked on he lifted her back into his arms. He bumped the door open, stepped in then kicked the door closed behind them. He was kissing her by the time he made it back to the bedroom. Her fingers tunneled into his hair as she gave herself to him.

His wife.

❦

Sun filtered in around the curtain. The diamond on her finger picked up the light and turned it into a rainbow of fire, but what held her attention was the firm, warm flesh under her hand. *Thayne. Her husband.* Emma was afraid to close her eyes, afraid that it all might be just a dream.

The large hand resting on her back moved. It stroked its way up to bury itself in her hair. She knew immediately it was going to tip her head up. It did and she met Thayne's gaze just before his lips closed over hers.

A groan escaped him echoed by one from her. "Good morning, Mrs. Rees." He proceeded to prove to her just how good a morning it was.

Later, they ate the breakfast delivered by room service out on the balcony again. They went for a swim in the pool below their room since no one else was in it. Afterwards, they returned to their room before strolling to the beach for one final walk on the sand and lunch. Emma enjoyed her last day in paradise, mostly because she was never out of contact with Thayne. Either they were holding hands or in each other's arms.

About a half hour before James was to arrive, Emma felt the tension start to build in Thayne, though outwardly he showed few signs. She caught him glance at the door then the window. She wished she could plead for more time, though she knew it was impossible. Thayne had to get the memory chip back to the states.

Emma watched him pace the room. He ended by the window. She placed her dress in the bag then went to stand behind him, wrapping her arms around his waist. His hands pressed down on hers, holding her to him. She leaned into his back.

They stood like that several minutes until he shifted his hand to her wrist and drew her around in front of him. He cocooned her in his arms, pressing her head to his chest. His lips brushed her hair.

"I wish we didn't have to leave." She returned the kiss on his neck.

"I wish I had you on the airplane, where I knew you were safe."

"It won't be long." She tried to comfort him.

"There's a lot of road between here and there."

"You don't think they can possibly know where we're at." She tried for logic.

"I didn't think they could find us on the island, but they did." The muscles in his arms tensed. "They may be watching the airport or the roads."

Emma leaned back to look up at him. "Then what's the plan?" She knew he would have one and didn't have to wait.

"I'd like you to wrap your hair up in a scarf at least until we get to security." He lifted his hand to catch a lock. "It really stands out." He smiled as he studied it.

"All right," Emma agreed easily. She would have cut it off if it would ease his stress.

"James will take us right to the terminal. We stay in the car until he gets our bag and brings it around to us. Another person will have already delivered our other bags."

"You know, they say don't carry on luggage you didn't pack yourself," she said jokingly.

"We'll go through our luggage inside before we check it in," Thayne answered totally serious. "Are you packed here?"

"Yes." Her lips twitched. Funny, her friends told her she tended to be over-cautious.

He looked down and forced a smile. "Sorry to sound so … paranoid, bossy and whatever. You're probably thinking; what have I gotten myself into."

"I'm thinking, I have myself a very smart, protective husband."

"I promise I'm not always like this. I just don't want anything else to happen to you and won't feel safe until we get home."

"Home sounds nice." She laid a palm to his cheek.

"It will be a home now. It's always been just a place where I keep my things." He kissed her hand then bent to kiss her lips.

The kiss continued until there was a knock on the door. Thayne motioned her back while he checked who it was. "It's James." He went to the bed and picked up the duffle bag and handed her his backpack.

"That's everything?" he asked, looking around the room.

"Yes. My purse is still in your backpack."

He led the way to the door, checking again before he opened it.

James went down the stairs first, Thayne brought up the rear. Once in the car, Thayne pulled out a scarf and Emma wrapped her hair into it then put on her sunglasses. "How do I look?"

"Like my own little spy." He interlocked their fingers,

keeping both hands against his thigh.

It only took them twenty five, uneventful minutes to reach the airport. Thayne's gaze constantly shifted to watch in front, behind, and around them. Just like he'd said, James pulled up in front, got out and came around with the duffle bag and stuff they'd bought the day before. He opened the door onto the sidewalk. Thayne took the bag as he got out, and pulled her out with him.

"Thank you." Emma barely got out before Thayne ushered her into the building and took her right to a security man.

"Hello. Can you help us? We had a break-in at the hotel we were staying at and had to leave quickly. Our luggage was left there, and it was to be sent over. Where would it have been delivered?"

The man looked them over, as if deciding whether to believe them but made a call. Emma watched as his expression changed. "Someone will come get you and take you to your luggage, if you just wait here."

A minute later an older Thai man in a security uniform approached them. "Mr. Rees?"

"Yes." Thayne held out his passport.

The man took it, looking it over before handing it back. "I am Jan, Chief of Security. If you will come with me, I have your luggage." He extended out his hand, directing them.

Thayne nodded and with his arm around her, fell in step with the man.

"I must say," Jan started. "This is most odd."

"Yes. I understand," Thayne answered easily. "It has been odd for us. A man started stalking my wife. We switched hotels after he broke into our room. Unfortunately, he found us again. I just got her out of there."

"I am sorry you have had such trouble on our island."

"It wasn't you island's fault. We loved it here. Just

someone saw her on the beach and took an interest in her."

The chief looked at her as if trying to see what would interest someone so much. Emma could just imagine how she looked with her hair wrapped in the scarf and the sunglasses. She almost laughed. She probably looked like those old actresses trying to go incognito.

The security man led them into a room off the main terminal, which was bare except for a large table and a couple of metal chairs. Their bags sat on the table. Jan held out his palm toward it.

"Thank you," Thayne said. "Is it okay if we check to make sure everything is here?"

"I would suggest it."

The man didn't leave, but the fact didn't seem to surprise Thayne. He released her and opened his bag. Emma followed his lead. Thayne pulled out all his belongings and went through everything before placing it all back inside before turning to help her. Emma noticed he checked around all the edges and seams carefully.

"Everything appears okay." Thayne helped her repack.

"I am glad." The security guard nodded from where he watched. "If you will come with me, I will take you through security."

Thayne shouldered the duffle and the chief took her suitcase leaving Emma to take the backpack. When Thayne took her by the elbow, Emma could feel the tension in him again, though outwardly he showed no signs. There was no trouble going through security with the new passport, though the chief did a double take when she removed her scarf and let her hair tumble down her back.

After passing through the scanners, Thayne turned to the chief. "Thank you for your assistance."

"You are most welcome. Your wife is, how they say, a stunning woman. It is no wonder she drew attention. It is most unfortunate it troubled your vacation.

"We enjoyed ourselves," Thayne answered.

"Yes," Emma added. "It was beautiful here. It will go down as my most favorite place." She smiled at Thayne.

"That is good. You may come back some time then." Jan said.

"We hope to." Emma turned to him. "Thank you for your help." She bowed her head slightly to the man.

He bowed back and walked away.

"I think you won him over," Thayne said as they made their way to their gate. "He no longer wonders why a man would become obsessed with you."

At first, Emma thought Thayne was teasing her, but a glance at him had her believing he was serious. "Thank you." She kissed his cheek. They settled down for the hour wait until they boarded the plane.

C3&O

After thirty hours on planes and in airports, it felt great to step off the plane in San Diego. Even with sleeping and watching movies the whole way, Emma was exhausted.

"What's the plan now?" she asked as they waited for their baggage.

"After we clear customs, we'll catch a cab to drop us at home. You can take a shower and relax while I run to the office and drop this off then I'll be back. We'll have dinner. I suggest a walk on the beach to keep us going to get back onto this time zone. Still, we'll have an early night. Tomorrow we'll go meet your parents and see how they take the news that you're married."

"They will like you."

"I hope so." He kissed her. "I plan to be around for a long time."

"Good. There's our bag." She tilted her head.

He smiled and turned to grab the duffle off the luggage belt.

"I wonder what Paige will say when I e-mail her that I married you."

"Probably that you're insane." He grinned.

"I don't think so. She knew I fell for you hard."

"You did?"

"Yes, though I tried not to."

He ran a finger along her cheek bone. "Why?"

"I was afraid."

He edged in closer to her. "Are you still?"

She shook her head. "I love you."

He dipped his head to kiss her. "I love you," he said the words against her lips then sealed them there with his. He eased back, but kept his arm around her.

A minute later, her suitcase dropped onto the conveyer belt. Thayne caught it up, and they headed out to catch a cab. A taxi headed for them, only to be cut off by a minivan cab that stopped at the curb directly in front of them.

Thayne caught her arm, stopping her. "No."

"Thayne." Emma felt him stiffen.

He waved the taxi driver on, but it remained there. The driver glared back.

"What's wrong?"

He shook his head. "Just—"

Someone bumped into Emma's back. Strong fingers locked onto her elbow. "Get in." What Thayne was saying was lost in the words said right behind her ear.

She opened her mouth to scream. Something pricked her side.

"Don't." The man hissed out and Emma felt a jab of pain.

Chapter Fifteen

She swallowed her cry as she recognized the knife man, but she made a sound loud enough Thayne spun toward her. His gaze went directly over her shoulder. The muscles around his eyes tightened. Fists clenched. His whole body went taunt.

"Tell your bodyguard not to make a scene. I can slip this knife between your ribs and be gone before you hit the ground." Emma knew Blade said it just loud enough for Thayne to hear. "Get in the van." He pushed her forward.

Emma glanced at Thayne. His lips compressed, but he nodded.

Emma took a step toward the van. The man behind her moved with her. A man in a business suit tried to step in front of them to get in, but a big man in a floral shirt cut him off coming in from the side.

"This one's taken." He blocked the businessman.

The man appeared like he was going to object for a moment then looked at the man, then over at her and backed away. Emma wanted to call out to him for help, but another jab in her side made her freeze. She then got a good look at the big man. Bruising around his eyes made him easily recognizable. He'd been one of the men on the island who'd tried to kidnap her. He was the one who had carried her over the hill.

She shifted her gaze to Thayne. A man stood directly behind him, similar to the one by her. This man was shorter, with dark, tight-cropped hair and a hard look around his eyes. No way would he ever be considered handsome but it was the hand in the pocket on his light jacket that made her truly nervous. Emma didn't doubt he had a gun. She wondered if he was from the island.

"You get in the car first." The man behind Thayne nudged him forward. Thayne looked back, shifting his gaze down to the hand in the pocket. Emma could see he was calculating every option.

The other man must have too. "You don't want to try it. I don't have a problem taking out a whole bunch of other people. Maybe that family there." The man tilted his head forward.

Emma looked at the young couple with two little girls dressed identically in pink shorts and tops. "Please don't hurt them." She couldn't keep back the words.

"Then get in."

Emma knew if they did, they were likely dead, but they couldn't be responsible for others dying. All she could do was put her faith in Thayne. She'd seen him fight before, but now he wasn't armed, and these men were. She watched Thayne step into the van.

"All the way over," the man behind him ordered.

Thayne slid over and the man got in behind him in the back seat. The guy with the knife nudged her forward again. Emma gasped at the prick on her skin. Thayne glared back but his jaw remained firmly shut.

The knife man slid into the seat right behind her. The big man closed the door. A second later, Emma heard the back hatch open, something, she figured was their luggage, was dropped inside. The back was closed, and the big man came around and climbed in the front passenger seat.

Panic hit her hard as they pulled away from the curb out into the slow traffic. She leaned into Thayne and felt his arm move, but he didn't try to put it around her. Instead, his muscles flexed and flexed again. She looked down and saw his cell-phone on the seat between them. A surge of hope filled her at seeing the screen lit.

"Is it all right if we fasten our seat belts?" Thayne asked.

Blade snickered. "Eddy, he doesn't trust your driving."

"He should worry about other things," Eddy said in return.

"Cut it," the man behind Thayne said. "Go ahead."

Thayne glanced from Emma to her seat. She fastened her seatbelt, using the motion to cover Thayne's movements. He pressed the phone into the seat between them as he did up the catch. She was grateful when he brought his arm up, this time he wrapped it around her.

⋘⋙

Thayne fumed silently at himself. He never imagined the possibility of an attack here. He'd been stupid to think just because they'd made it back to the states that everything was over. His only consolation was Matt hadn't considered it either. If he had, he would've met them at the airport with a team, but he hadn't even sent a car.

Thayne couldn't even shake his head in disgust. He clenched his jaw, but forced himself to stay relaxed. It was a good thing he was getting out of the business, because he'd definitely lost his edge. He wasn't totally washed up yet though, and he had to get Emma out of the situation.

He was aware of her tucked in next to him. Her hands were locked together in her lap, but she was holding it together, though he could feel the faint tremors in her body. He placed his hand over hers and squeezed.

She looked up at him. He could see her fear, but there was trust in her eyes. She opened her hands and wrapped her fingers around his. She made a little glance at his phone tucked down between them.

At least, he'd turned his phone on when they'd landed to let Matt know they were on the ground. It hadn't been hard for him to call the last number called by touch. He didn't know who had answered. He just knew there was a connection. So as long as it wasn't disconnected, they could easily be tracked.

"Where you taking us?" Thayne asked as they headed north on the freeway.

"Not far." One of them men behind him answered.

"What's this all about?"

"For you, probably nothing, but for your girlfriend, she has something we want," the man answered.

"Yeah, you picked the wrong woman to get involved with, sucker," Big Boy in the front seat said. "Hope she was worth it." He snickered.

Thayne ignored him. "What's that?"

"None of your business," Blade snapped and smacked the back of Thayne's head.

Emma gasped.

For a second, Thayne saw stars, though it wasn't a hard hit.

"Not yet," the other man in back said.

"I owed him that."

Thayne was ready for another blow, but it didn't come.

"Just because he bested you idiots," the man, who Thayne figured was in charge, said derisively.

"Hey, we weren't expecting him." Big Boy slouched a little.

"And what about when you tried to snatch her off the island?" the boss came back. "I shouldn't have had to be here, to even get involved."

The car fell silent. Thayne glanced down. He could barely make the phone out between them on the seat, but he could see enough to know it was still connected. They just needed time but that was something Thayne was worried they were running out of.

As if to confirm the thought, the van exited the freeway and went a short ways into an industrial area. Thayne didn't like the sight of warehouse after warehouse and limited people around. Carefully, he slid his hand free from Emma's and reached for the phone. Pulling it out, he tilting it up just enough to check the connection.

Relief poured through his body that it was. He forced the phone deeper down into the seat. They had a chance as long as they weren't separated from the vehicle. He just couldn't risk leaving the phone on him. As soon as they stopped they'd be searched. The only reason they hadn't been so far was there was no way to do it at the airport without drawing attention.

The van pulled up to one of the warehouses and stopped in front of a large metal garage door. Big boy got out and entered the building through a small side door.

"What's this? Artey's Imports," Thayne said the name clearly, trying not to over stress it.

Whether the men would've answered, there wasn't any time as the garage door opened and the van drove inside. As soon as they were clear, the door closed behind them. Blade stood and reached to open the sliding door on the van before they even stopped. The boss followed him out.

"Out," the boss ordered as he turned back to the van, a gun appearing in his hand.

Emma looked back at him. Thayne nodded. "Slowly."

"No talking," the driver ordered.

Emma jumped, but very slowly turned to the opening. Thayne used the cover of her movement to force his phone farther into the seat. As Emma stepped down, Blade grabbed her and pulled her away from the door toward the front of the van.

"Okay, now you," the boss said. "Slowly," he repeated what Thayne had told her, letting him know he'd heard.

Thayne slid to the edge of the seat and extended his leg down until it touched the ground then stood.

"Up front." Boss motioned with the tip of the gun.

Thayne raised his hands up, palms out and walked slowly to Emma. He wanted their attention off the inside of the van as soon as possible. He felt a wave of relief when he heard the door slide closed, and the driver get out.

Thayne let his gaze float over the interior of the building. Rows of stacked crates stretched out in front of them. Around the walls of the building, metal shelves reached to the ceiling, containing smaller crates. The place was a maze, which could be good for him and Emma if he could get them into it.

Turning his attention back to the men, he found the boss focused on him. Thayne ignored the attention, casting his eyes to Emma while he calculated the distance from her to the closest box. Ten feet. Not bad but still a lot of space. What he'd need was a diversion.

"Hands on the hood. Feet spread," the boss ordered.

Thayne turned slowly, taking the position. Emma followed his movements. She'd stayed close, but he also noticed she didn't crowd him. She was giving him room if he needed to move. *Good girl.* He tried to send her the message mentally, but all he could really do was catch her gaze and hope she understood.

Big boy stepped up behind them and started patting him down first, taking his watch, wallet and passport. Identifying items, Thayne realized. Emma let out a small gasp when the man started on her. Thayne had to steal himself not to react to the man's beefy hands running down her body. He wanted to smash his fist into the man for laying a hand on her. *Timing,* he said the word in his mind.

"She's clean," Big Boy said, backing up.

"All right. Turn around," the boss again gave the order.

Thayne let his hand brush over Emma's arm as he turned. He longed to take hold of her, but he had to be free, be ready to move if an opportunity presented itself.

"Get the luggage." The boss didn't look at his men. It wasn't necessary. The driver and Big Boy walked around to the back of the car.

Thayne met the boss's gaze as the man stared at him.

He kept his gun pointed directly at Emma but only letting his eyes flick briefly to her.

Blade stood off to the side. There was a bruise on the man's chin that made his scar stand out.

The two men came back and dumped their bags on the ground.

The boss shifted his gaze to Emma. "If you tell us where it is, it will go easier for you."

"I—I don't know what you're talking about." Her voice trembled, but she remained calm.

The man studied her.

Emma's trembling was visible, as was the quick glance she sent his way before dropping her gaze to the floor.

"You idiots!" The boss's sharp exclamation echoed through the building. "She doesn't have it."

The other men jerked.

"She's the one who received it," Big Boy said with certainty.

"That may be, but if she did, it was by accident. Wasn't it?" The man shifted and looked directly at him. Thayne held his gaze, happy to have the attention off Emma.

"Was he there?" the boss snapped.

"Yeah, I'd been watching him. I figured it might have been him from the first, but he didn't make the pickup. It was her," Big Boy said defensively.

"And when did our hero show up?"

"Well." Big boy hesitated. "He was on the same boat. They ran into each other when going back for departure call. He sat at the same table at lunch but didn't hang around with her. He was also in the same van that returned her to her hotel, but he didn't get off there. Only her and her friend got off."

The boss nodded, clearly thinking. "Search him again." This time he nodded to Blade.

There was a slight swagger in the man's stride as he

came toward Thayne. "Turn around." Thayne caught a glint in the man's eye and figured he was in for a touch of pay back, but turned keeping his hands out, placing them on the hood then spread his feet wider, just not too wide.

Blade jabbed an elbow in his back. Thayne fell against the hood, glad at least it wasn't Blade's knife.

Thayne turned his head to look back over his shoulder, seeing the fear in Emma's eyes. He said nothing while Blade patted him down and turned his pockets inside out.

"Nothing," Blade said just before Thayne heard a soft snicker. He felt a tiny jab as the knife caught his skin, which Thayne was sure was intentional, before the sharp edge sliced through the material.

Another gasp slipped from Emma, and she started to reach for him but thankfully froze.

"Where's his phone?" Blade blurted out, obviously just remembering it. "He had a phone in the market."

"Check the van." Boss ordered. Big Boy went to the sliding door, while the driver knelt by the backpack, opening the zippers and rummaging through. He'd just pulled out Emma's tablet and her phone, when Big Boy said. "I found…"

Thayne went into action the instant Blade shifted his attention to his cohort. He dipped his head away from the knife as he shoved his elbow hard into Blades chin. Blade's head snapped back, and the man dropped. Thayne was already on the move before Blade hit the ground.

Grabbing Emma's hand, he pulled her toward the closest stack of crates. She moved easily with him. Ducking in behind the stack, she matched his stride.

The driver, with his hands in the pack, was too slow to react. The boss, who had looked at Big Boy when he spoke, turned back and fired wildly. The shots buried deep into a crate several feet behind Emma. Thayne didn't slow, running full out with her. He pulled them between two crates into a new aisle, heading deeper into the warehouse.

"Stay with the van. Make sure they don't try to get out that way. You there, Eddy, with me."

"What about the phone?" The voice was Blade's.

Thayne heard a clatter.

"He won't be making any calls."

Silence swept over the warehouse. Thayne slowed their pace. Thanks to the fact they were both wearing soft-soled shoes, they moved quietly.

Thayne led her around several more stacks. They ended up next to the shelves. Thayne halted and listened. Emma clung to his arm. The scrape of a heel on concrete revealed the location of the boss. At the sound of heavy breathing, Thayne guessed it was Big Boy with him. He wondered where Blade was. Probably the far side in case they had tried to make their way there.

Thayne looked around for options. He hoped Matt had their location and help was on the way. He just wasn't going to risk his and Emma's lives on it. That meant he had to take care of the men, which meant he had to get Emma somewhere safe. He turned and studied the shelving unit. A few feet down, there was a gap between two crates.

"In there." He motioned to the space.

He could see Emma wanted to argue but she didn't. She turned to the side and slid between the stacks, ducking in between the crates and the wall, totally disappearing.

Thayne hurried down the aisle a little farther, then ducked between crates and out onto the next aisle. He didn't want to get too far from Emma in case they discovered her, but he also wanted to lead them away.

As Thayne saw it, he had two choices. He either needed to keep the men busy until help arrived, or he had to take them out. He had no doubt that as soon as they got the chip, he and Emma were dead. He'd bet their bodies would be loaded up in one of the crates and shipped out, either to be buried in the desert or taken out to sea and dumped. None of the options appealed to him, and no one was going to hurt Emma.

He froze at the sound ahead and to the left. Backing up several feet, he ducked back into a space between two crates. The cramped area would afford him little room to maneuver, but it was a good hiding place.

There was another scuff on the cement floor. This one closer. Thayne held his breath and waited, resisting the urge to look out. Only a couple seconds passed before he heard the man clearly moving his way. He didn't know who but didn't think it was the knife man with a cat-like grace. There was also no faint click of a man's dress shoes that indicated the boss.

That left Big Boy. Thayne would have preferred to face him last after taking out the gun carrying boss and Blade first. He'd just have to be fast and quiet. Thayne barely brought the image of the large man up in his mind when Big Boy passed his hiding place, not even glancing his way.

Thayne waited until he was out of view before moving. Stepping into the aisle about five feet behind the large man, Thayne closed the distance in less than a second.

Big Boy detected him at the last instant, but Thayne struck before he could even begin to turn. Thayne slammed his fists down on either side of the man's head. Big Boy dropped but Thayne wasn't done. Still holding Big Boy's head, Thayne shifted around, bringing the man's face down as he brought his knee up. Thayne caught and lowered the unconscious body to the floor, minimizing the noise.

He remained tense, listening for anyone heading his way. Satisfied it was clear, he pulled off his belt and used it to secure the large, beefy arms behind Big Boy's back, then back-tracked to where he'd left Emma.

CBEO

Emma waited and listened, fear beating in her heart. She wanted to go after Thayne, but she knew it was best for him that she remain hidden and not distract him. At a faint scuff on the floor she froze, when the sound came again, it didn't sound close. After a second, silence once more descended.

She held her breath, listening. Nothing followed. She eased forward slightly, trying to peer around the smaller crate stacked on the larger one which she hid behind. She got a good view down the aisle toward where the doors were. The way was empty.

She moved to the other side but couldn't see as much. She craned her head a bit more and caught a movement and pulled back. Holding her breath, she looked again, zeroing in on the man but relaxed. It was Thayne. He glided along the row of crates, angled slightly to the side.

He paused when he got close, his eyes going right to her. A tight smile gave a hint of a crescent to his lips. He held up his hand to stay her.

She nodded that she understood his meaning. He tipped his head back at her, starting to move down the row toward the front. She shifted to follow his movements. He passed her position and covered half the distance when he froze and pressed back against a stack of crates.

Emma jumped and almost screamed when the smaller man whipped around the corner, a knife slashing where Thayne's neck would have been if he hadn't pulled back.

Thayne thrust up his arm, driving the hand holding the knife away. Blade drove his fist into Thayne's side. Thayne countered back, driving his own fist hard into the man's stomach. Blade staggered back. Thayne went in closing the space between them as he brought his other fist up to the knife man's chin.

Emma was so locked on watching the fight she almost missed the movement directly in front of her. She jerked back, but the man didn't react, too intent on the fight going on ahead. Panic hit Emma at the sight of the gun in the man's hand pointed at Thayne.

Emma glanced at Thayne, but his attention was

focused on Blade and the knife they grappled over. She looked back at the gunman in time to see him lift his gun a touch higher, lining up his shot. Another glance at the fight, she saw Thayne break the man's hold and smash his fist up to the underside of the man's jaw.

Emma knew the instant Thayne won, the man would shoot him. Placing her hands on the smaller crate, Emma shoved with all her weight. The crate moved easier than she calculated. Losing her balance, Emma came down against the lower crate making it topple, crashing down on the gunman, taking him to the floor with her sprawled on top.

Sounds of shots and the clatter of falling crates echoed through the building then faded into a cascade of shouts. It took Emma a second to separate all the noise as panic filled her.

Thayne! She pushed herself up, looking for him

"Freeze. Get your hands up." The words punctuated her mind first.

She froze, her eyes locked on Thayne.

He knelt on the floor by Blade, seemly totally relaxed now. Turning her way, he stood and walked calmly toward her. Stopping just above her, he extended out his hand. His eyes burned with fire, but Emma felt no fear of being consumed. She placed her hand in his. In one fluid movement, he pulled her up and into his heat. His mouth descended to claim hers, sealing her to him.

Emma became lost in him, until the sound of a man clearing his throat loudly finally penetrated her mind.

"I thought we were supposed to be rescuing you." A man wearing a bulletproof vest and carrying a gun said when Thayne lifted his head and looked at him.

"You took your sweet time," Thayne returned.

Emma dropped her head to Thayne's shoulder, relieved by his relaxed state.

"Yeah, well." The man shrugged.

"Yeah, easy pickup." Thayne's voice fairly crackled

with energy. "That guy's dead." Thayne nodded to Blade. "The guy there hit him instead of me when Emma knocked the crates on him. Don't know how he is. There's another guy a couple aisles over, tied up and unconscious where I left him."

The man nodded and repeated the information into a microphone hanging down by his cheek. Then he smiled and walked toward them. "This must be Emma Stephens." He held out his hand to her.

"Emma Rees," Thayne said firmly. "Emma, my boss and supposed friend, Matt Harding."

"Nice to meet you." Emma automatically stuck out her hand.

"Don't I get to kiss the bride?" He smiled down, a devilish glint sparking in his eyes. "I have a few stories to tell you about this guy. The newest one was just last week."

"Matt." Thayne's voice rose threateningly.

The man continued as if he didn't hear him. "He was in my office and swore he didn't need a woman in his life, and he was never getting married again."

"Matt!"

"He's so easy to get a reaction from, and I so like that you laid him low."

Emma got the feeling he was being totally facetious and felt herself warm. She relaxed more into Thayne's arms. Now the danger was over, she was exhausted from their ordeal on top of their long trip home.

"You know," Matt spoke again, looking directly at Thayne, "you have something I need. If you want to hand it over, I'll take you home as soon as you're checked out by the paramedics."

"I don't need the paramedics, but I'm more than ready to get rid of this thing." Thayne rubbed his hip.

✑

It was almost two hours later, after they'd given their statements and answered all the questions before Matt dropped them off at Thayne's house. Emma had cuddled against his shoulder fighting to stay awake during the car ride, but at the arrival at her new home, her excitement spiked. She was stunned at the sight of the two-story stucco and brick home with a three-car garage. It was bigger than she'd thought. In fact, it was quite large by southern California standards. It sat on a slight rise surrounded by a lawn that was in need of being mowed. There was a rock tier with a couple palm trees and azalea bushes.

"What do you think Mrs. Rees?" Thayne asked, helping her out of the car.

"Beautiful, but I think we could use some flowers."

"Whatever you wish." Thayne slid an arm around her waist. "But, not today. I'm exhausted. I just want to go in to bed. I'm afraid we'll have to save that walk on the beach for another day." He nuzzled her neck.

"That's okay." She leaned back into him and sighed with pleasure. They stood there as one, staring at the home that held their future.

Matt wordlessly lifted their suitcases out of the car, placing them on the walk then got back in his car and drove away, leaving them on their own.

"Shall we go in?" Thayne motioned.

"Yes, please."

Emma took the backpack and the new duffle while he carried his duffle and her suitcase. He led her up the front walk. On the step, he put the bags down and entered a combination into a key pad.

"Stay here," he said. Opening the door, he placed the bags inside then took the bags from her, dropping them in by the suitcase.

He turned back to her, a gleam in his eyes. "Mrs. Rees, welcome home." He wrapped his arms around her, kissed her, and then lifted her up in his arms, stepping over the threshold.

Emma caught a glimpse of a high ceiling and a

staircase curving up on one side before Thayne was kissing her again, and she became lost in the sensation of floating as he headed up the stairs. At the top of the stairs, he ended the kiss and turned to give her a view looking over the balcony.

"Thayne, this is beautiful."

"Thank you. As soon as I walked into this house, I knew it was my home. It's kind of like when you fell into my arms. I knew you were the one for me."

"You really knew?"

"I did. I didn't want to, but I did."

"Matt said a week ago you said you didn't want a woman in your life?"

"It's true." He cocked up an eyebrow. "I didn't think being married to me was safe."

Emma saw a flicker of shadow cross his face and raised her fingers to his cheek. She stroked lightly, as if to brush away any lingering self-recrimination.

She thought about what she'd been through. "I don't regret one moment of the last week. Well, except maybe when I was upset with you, but there will probably be times that will happen again in the future. That's part of life. I guess what I'm saying is – you'll just have to always be there to rescue me, because I love you, and am willing to face anything just for a single day with you." She stretched up and kissed him.

His arms held her tight to him when she leaned back.

"I would move heaven and earth to find you and keep you safe."

There was no doubting his words. Joy filled her. "I wonder what my parents will think about having a spy in the family."

He shook his head. "I'm just an engineer, now."

"No – you're my spy." She kissed him.

A second later, she was lifted back into his arms and carried into his – correction – their bedroom.

ALYSIA S. KNIGHT

About the Author

I grew up in a small town in Wyoming loving the outdoors, sports, art, and reading Hardy Boys books. After reading them all at least a half dozen times, I started writing my own stories.

Thirty years ago I married a wonderful, honorable man. I'm mother of five children and grandmother of six boys. I love traveling. Through my husband's work and vacations, I have visited much of the United States, all over Eastern Europe, Canada, Mexico, China, Thailand, Cambodia and Australia, giving me many intriguing locations and experiences for my stories.

I am a storyteller. I write the classic hero story because I think there's a need for more heroes, love, and adventure in our lives. I'm not out to change the world with my writing; I'm just hoping to make your day a little better.

Hope you enjoy.
Alysia S. Knight

Please feel free to visit me through my website:

WWW.ALYSIASKNIGHT.COM

www.ingramcontent.com/pod-product-compliance
Lightning Source LLC
Chambersburg PA
CBHW021958190626
46808CB00017B/2257